HER RIGHT

BOOK TWO OF NEW BEGINNINGS

Kaden Shay

Supposed Crimes LLC • Matthews, North Carolina

Her Right

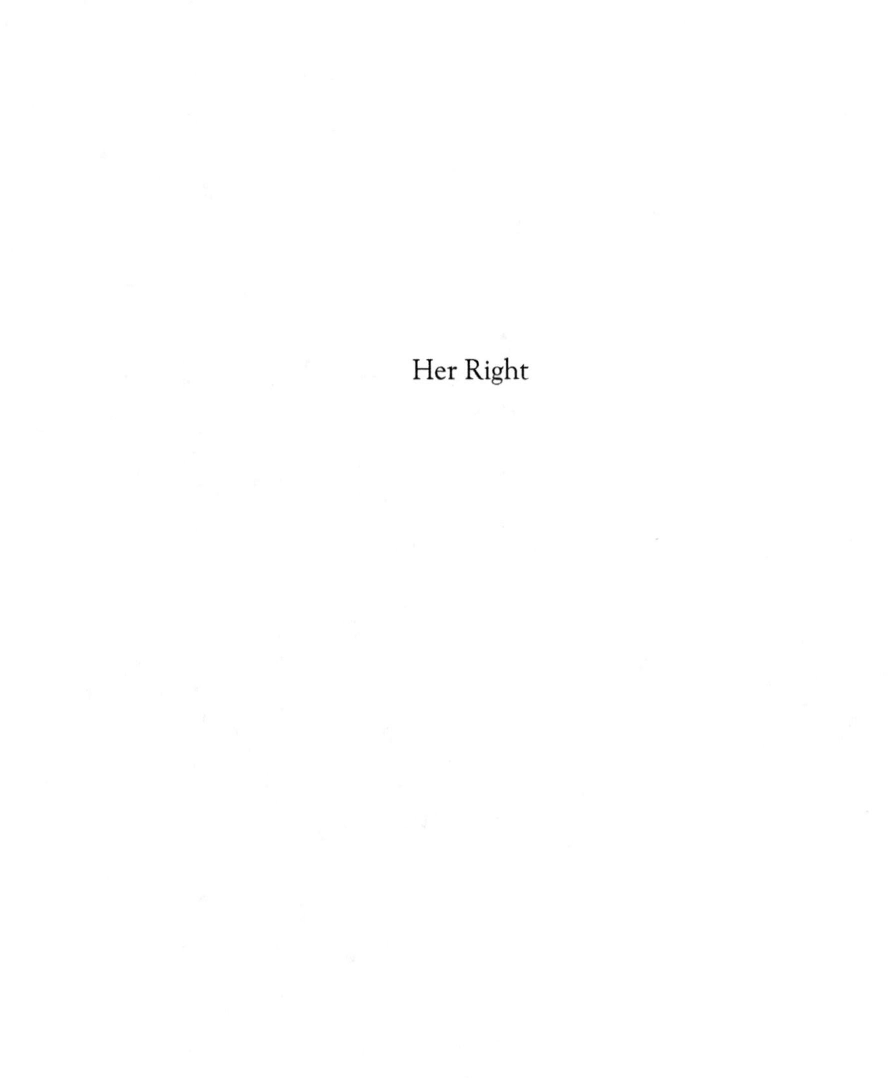

CHAPTER ONE

I WOKE suddenly and pushed myself upright in the darkness of the master bedroom, the chill of the December air wafting in through the open bedroom window and cooling my sweat-soaked skin. Another nightmare had ripped me from my sleep. I'd been having them every couple nights ever since my father had shown up at Abbey and Kyle's ceremony three months earlier. He'd had yet to make good on his promise to take my new pack from me, but that didn't help me sleep any better. I felt a hand on my shoulder and the contact pulled me back into myself and the present moment as my eyes focused on my room in the darkness.

Just a hint of silver moonlight spilled through the open curtains, it would be a new moon in less than a week. The light that was coming into the room allowed my sharpened eyesight to see the room clearly as I turned my gaze to the woman beside me. I gave her a weak smile, attempting to reassure her that I was alright, even though she would know I wasn't.

"Another one?" I just nodded and watched as her brows knit down in concern before she wrapped her arm around me and pulled me in closer. Poor Frost had been dealing with these nightmares for months now. When it wasn't these rather horrific ones about my father then it was the terribly vivid memories of my challenge with her brother months earlier. As much as the man had deserved what had happened to him, deep down I was still unnerved by what I had done. I let out a heavy sigh and leaned against my mate, wishing that we could just have one full week of uninterrupted sleep. I was starting to feel ragged and worn and the bullshit the new pack was pulling since word of my father's challenge got out was wearing my nerves thin.

Freddie was treading on thin ice and I was only one wrong comment away from taking his head off, literally. Greg and one of the other displaced enforcers were becoming a problem and I was being backed into a corner with them. It wouldn't be long before I would be forced to either kill them or banish them, neither of those was an option I liked. We had so much going on, so many things that needed to be handled on a daily basis and I just felt like I was spread too thin these days. Shane, the youngest of my four brothers, had stayed in Rider territory since the beating our father had laid on him the night of Abbey's bonding. He had decided to leave our father's pack and join ours and I hadn't given a second thought to allowing it, whether my father liked it or not.

Since then, my oldest brother Dante, his mate and their young son had also defected and joined our new pack. The four of them lived together now and I just hoped that the two brothers that had stayed were handling my father's temper well. By leaving, Dante had given up his chance to lead the Clipper pack and if anything happened to my father, the task would fall to Brandon. I hoped he had what it would take to lead, to be different, because I knew that eventually my father would make good on his threat. That led me right back into dangerous territory, into thoughts that I had been trying to avoid, but that kept creeping their way into my mind. I was only eighteen, only a teenage girl and I had no experience with any of this.

What made me think that I could manage something so huge, something so far out of my comfort level? Had I lost my mind? Was I just dreaming when I had thought that Frost and I could actually do this thing, that we could turn this pack around and lead them? What if I couldn't live up to the promises I had made to the pack, or if I managed to make things even worse than they had been before? I was so full of questions and doubts and I was rapidly approaching the point of breakdown, something I knew my mate could not only sense, but see in me.

"What if he was right, Frost?"

"Who?"

"My father... What if he was right and I can't do this? What if I just can't handle running a pack." I was staring at my legs where they were pulled up, crossed pretzel-style as I leaned against Frost. I felt her lean away for a moment then her bedside lamp clicked on, washing the room in a flood of pale yellow light. A moment later, her hands were on my cheeks and she was forcing me to look up, giving me no choice but to meet her eyes. As they always had, the sight of those pale purple irises stopped my heart for a moment and made my breath catch. She moved her left hand enough to brush some hair from my face so she could see my eyes better and then kissed the tip of my nose. A small smile tugged up the left corner of my lips and she returned the small gesture before she spoke.

"Listen to me. Don't let him get in your head, okay? You can do this, we can do this. Yes, there have been some issues, but there are bound to be disputes in a situation like this. The only real issues are Freddie and the old enforcers, right?" I nodded a little bit in response since she was right, they were the major issues within our new pack that needed dealt with. "Okay, well, Freddie is actually easy to deal with. Banish him, Kyndle. Killing him will make him a martyr to those in the pack that believe his crap. Banishing him makes a statement, remove him from the pack, those that feel like following him, will, then they aren't our problem anymore.

As for the enforcers, Greg and Daniel are the only two still giving us any problems on the matter. Oscar, Chad and Parker have fallen in line and are doing what you told them to do. My suggestion, if you want it..." She paused to allow me to answer her on whether I wanted her opinion on the matter, which was ludicrous, that answer would always be yes.

"Of course I want it..."

"I figured you did, but you know I'll always ask..." I just nodded because it was true, she would never just assume that I wanted her opinion, despite the fact that I saw her as my equal, my partner in this, she would always make sure. "Parker has not only fallen in line, but has been willing to settle back into just being a member of the pack, he's given the least resistance to your choices since you stripped his rank and has even offered his help in training replacement enforcers of your choice. Reinstate him, give him back his rank and his title and allow him to train two or three new enforcers. Show the rest of the pack that you're fair, you stripped them, yes, but you are also willing to give those ranks back given proper respect and behavior." I couldn't even say anything to that, I just smiled and leaned in to give my mate the kiss that she deserved.

As I leaned back, she smiled, but then gave me a look like she didn't know what I had done that for.

"You always know what I should do. You may not have the blunt dominance for this pack leadership deal baby, but you've definitely got the brains. You're right, Parker has been nothing but helpful for the last few weeks and I think he's earned another chance. I may have no choice but to deal with Greg though, maybe if I remove him, Daniel will fall into line, if not, he can leave too." She gave me a nod and then pulled me in close against her side and gave me a tight squeeze that made me wrap my arms around her and hug her back. She always knew how to make me feel better, how to put everything into perspective so that it made sense. Even without all the other things I adored about her, all the other amazing things that she had going for her, that one trait in itself was enough to make me love her.

"Let's get back to sleep sweetie, we have a couple hours before we need to be awake. The pack meeting is coming up, we'll handle all of this then." I just gave her a small nod before she leaned over and flipped off the lamp then settled down into the bed beside me. I reached out for her in the dark, needing to close the small gap of open space between us on the mattress. She shifted over closer as I settled onto my back so she could cuddle up against my right side, her head on my shoulder and her arm across my stomach. We drifted back into a, thankfully, nightmare free sleep that lasted until the sun rose and our alarm went off to tell us it was time to start our day.

The remodel on the old house had been done for a while and we had really settled in and made it home, a sanctuary, it was our refuge. Our day was spent cleaning, running errands and then lounging in the living room in front of the fireplace. We were taking advantage of the calm before the storm, the lazy moments we could grab before the pack meeting the next day. There was bound to be an outcry, some would argue that we were changing too much, that I was being too harsh, but I knew what needed to be done. I couldn't allow the challenges to my still new authority in the pack to continue or they would only spread and become worse. Two or three wolves I could deal with, I could remove the problem and make an example out of them. Half the pack turning on Frost and I, no, that would be too much for us to handle without some serious backup, backup that we didn't have at the moment.

I had been tolerating the comments, the insubordination and

the downright rude attitudes of this handful of males for eight months now and I was over it. It had to stop before it escalated and I could feel that we were rapidly approaching that point. I was determined to go into that meeting with my mind clear, my choices made and as relaxed as I possibly could be given the circumstances. That meant sticking to our usual routine and then having a nice night together, something that I fully intended on working n for the sake of my sanity. I knew I had been short tempered, moody and exhausted the last few months and I felt the need to make it up to Frost. The mental link that we both knew was bound to form had begun to show itself the last few weeks and she was slowly working toward being able to tell exactly what I was thinking. It was a little unnerving, but at the same time, a bit relaxing since there were times when I wanted to tell her what I was thinking or feeling but couldn't find the words. Lately, I rarely needed the words, she just knew and that took a lot of the pressure off.

Our day ended on a relaxed peak and I had a wonderfully romantic night with Frost, spent in front of the fireplace we had added to the master bedroom as many of our nights had ended the last two months. We were already considering heating the pool so that next winter we could actually use the thing, which would be amazing. We had taken a dip in the hot tub for about an hour but eventually decided to head in once the sun began to set and a deep chill settled in, even around the heated water. My sleep that night was, thankfully, uneventful and dream free as far as I could remember, allowing me the restful night of deep sleep I needed to deal with the pack the next day.

CHAPTER TWO

I EASED back out of sleep with the golden rays of the morning sun falling across my face and thoughts of the pack drifting into my mind. Frost was still asleep beside me so I glanced over at the clock and found that the alarm wouldn't go off for another ten minutes. I decided to keep still and allow her the extra minutes of sleep, she would need it to make it through the day ahead of us. I was new to this, but this was her pack, had been her family and friends for her entire life and they were turning on her now. I knew that had to be hard on her, had to be ripping at her heart in a way that my father's challenge had ripped away at mine. I got so lost in my thoughts that those last few minutes passed more quickly than I expected them to. The alarm startled me when it went off and I jumped slightly, jarring Frost where she was still nestled against me and waking her up. "Sorry. Was lost in my head and the alarm scared me." She just gave me a sleepy smile, shook her head as she yawned and then leaned up to kiss my forehead.

"It's fine, honey. Good morning."

"Good morning gorgeous."

I smiled at her as her cheeks flushed a slight pink and then chuckled as she turned over, using her hair to cover her face as she slipped out of the bed. I utilized the few seconds it took her to cross over to the closet by getting in a stretch that made my back pop. I let out a sigh at the feel of it and then slid from the bed and joined my mate in the closet to begin getting ready for the day. We milled around in the closet for a few minutes, both trying to decide what to wear and each asking for the others opinion here and there. We needed to be prepared for anything, confident but comfortable and the clothes needed to be ones we didn't mind losing if we had to shift suddenly without notice. Once clothes were picked out, we made our way to the bathroom to shower and get ourselves together.

Showering with someone was supposed to save water, whoever had that idea had never been in a shower with Frost and I. We tended to get sidetracked easily and almost every shower we'd been in together had lasted long enough for the water to run cold. Finally cleaned up, dried off, dressed and put together we were ready to head out to our pack meeting. We had started having these at least once a month, they were needed since this pack had a lot of issues to work through. There was no denying that it would take time, no doubt that we had a lot working against us but I had every confidence now, thanks to Frost and her pep talk a couple nights before, that we could make it work. We took our time having breakfast, taking every moment that we had alone before the chaos began.

These meetings always lasted through lunch and dinner and often well into the evenings, but we didn't dare cancel them. Breakfast finished, dishes rinsed and in the dishwasher, we finally gathered up the few things that we would need at the meeting and headed out. The pack had a meeting hall that was large enough for everyone, but before we took over, it was rarely used. Pack gatherings were rare under the last two Alpha's but we had every intention of fixing that and letting the pack know that we were a family now.

I stepped into the hall with Frost at my side and paused long enough to take in the room in front of me. About half the pack was already gathered and the rest would make their appearances by the time the meeting started in about twenty minutes. The first couple meetings we had held I had attempted to be present before the rest of the pack, wanting to make a statement and all that jazz. That had proven itself to be an impossibility since I had learned that there were pack members that would arrive with the sunrise and just wait for us. I was dedicated to making this work, to making this pack everything that it could be, but I wasn't insane. I liked my sleep, I needed my sleep and I wouldn't be any good to anyone half dead and dozing off every few minutes. So I just remained content in sleeping in and showing up twenty or thirty minutes before the announced time set for each meeting. It seemed to sit just fine with most of the pack and the ones that did make waves about it were about to be dealt with.

I aimed a friendly nod toward the corner to a couple of the younger pack members that I assumed were already present because there wasn't much better to do just then. They nodded back and went back to their various activities as I continued to scan those already present. The teenagers in the pack would benefit most from the changes that Frost and I were trying to implement and we well knew it. We had already won over a majority of them, simply because we were young and we understood where they were coming from. The rest of those present were at the opposite end of the age spectrum, the elder members of the pack. They were the ones, outside Freddie and Greg that had been the most outspoken against the idea of me being their new Alpha. I had the feeling that the objections had ranged from the same objection my father had, a female leading a pack, to the fact that my mate happened to be female as well. I had given up trying to help anyone get over that second point, they accepted it or they didn't and I wasn't about to get into fights about it.

I felt Frost's hand slip into mine and I smiled as she stepped forward and gave me a little tug to get me moving. Once I was walking, we made our way to the table on the small raised platform near the eastern end of the room. This was the Alpha's table and it was where Frost, myself, Abbey and Kyle sat during these gatherings, presenting a united, if small, front to the rest of the pack. I pulled Frost's chair for her, let her get seated and then settled into my own chair as Abbey stepped into the building, Kyle in tow. I gave her a wave and she smiled and waved back before heading for the table then taking the seat to my left. I always had Frost on my right, Abbey to my left, each one of the two hands that I couldn't function without. The other three began chatting as I focused on the room before me, watching intently as the rest of the pack slowly filtered into the space and filled it. Conversations filled the space, each group having their own little meetings before the larger one began, deciding what they needed to speak about during this time.

I finally looked away from the room of werewolves and glanced down at my watch, surprised to find that it was time to begin already. I stood and cleared my throat to get everyone's attention, thankful that was all it took to quiet the room. With our keen hearing, even in human form, it rarely took much to get attention refocused which meant the meeting could start on time without any shouting for things to quiet down.

"Welcome everyone. Glad to see you all here again." I took a moment to let my eyes flicker toward Frost, just long enough to catch her small nod that getting the messy things out of the way first was best. "Before we open the floor for pack questions this month..." The words were strong and steady as I turned my attention back to the full room before me. "I have some business that needs handling. I understand that this may be a rather messy way to begin a pack meeting but it needs to be done before anything else is brought to our attention. Freddie, Greg, will you please step to the front of the room..."

I waited as the two males stood and approached our table, a buzz of hushed comments sweeping through the room. Once they were standing in front of me, Freddie looking a bit like a scolded puppy and Greg sporting a smirk I'd have liked to slap right off his face, I took a deep breath and continued.

"It's been eight months since Frost and I returned and took over leadership of this pack. Over those months the two of you have done absolutely nothing to help further the pack, to help make it better. All you've done is disrespect me, disrespect my mate and challenge my choices and my authority. I have been more patient than I probably should have been given the things you have both said and done and that ends now." I paused to allow a hushed whisper ripple through the room and then swept my gaze over the crowd, regaining their attention before I continued. "Punishment will be handed down here and now and there will be no arguments from either of you." Freddie's eyes went wide, almost as if he couldn't believe what he was hearing and I saw a flicker of fear behind them.

Greg, on the other hand, looked angry, his glare leveled on me and if looks could kill, well, I'd probably be dead a few times over. "As of today, you're both banished." An uproar went up through the pack, not every member having an issue with what I had just said, but enough to make a decent commotion. "Quiet, everyone!" I didn't shout but the words were sharp enough that the point was made and the room settled down seconds later. "Any of you who think that this punishment is too harsh, you have two options, bring it up with me rationally later, or leave with these two. That said, I'd like both of you to remove yourselves from this hall, gather your things and be out of pack territory by sun down. The rest of this meeting no longer concerns you."

Greg looked like he was about to argue, but I turned a glare on him and stepped over into his space, the height of the platform allowing me to look down just slightly to meet his eyes. "You have been officially banned, by pack law, you can argue all you want, but you still have to leave. Make this easier and just go, fight me and I swear, I'll win, I don't want to kill you, Greg, but I will." The words were just loud enough for the two males before me to hear and while he still looked as mad as a hornet, he turned on his heel and stormed out of the hall, the older male right behind him.

I took a moment to compose myself and make sure that Greg wouldn't storm back in before I took a deep, steadying breath and addressed the pack again. "I know my choice may seem harsh, but I can't have the safety and well-being of this pack jeopardized. Daniel, come here." He stepped forward and I looked at him for a moment, allowing him to wonder what I was about to say to him. "You've backed Greg the last few months. I'm giving you a choice now, stand down and follow my rules, or join him. You have a week to prove yourself to me. Step back." He gave me a shaky nod and then slipped back to his seat looking a little dejected and I hoped that Greg had been the driving force there. I put my hands up to settle the flurry of questions that started flying my way, wanting to get a couple other things handled before the third degree started. "Parker, would you step up here please?" My tone was lighter this time, the smile back on my face, but Parker still looked a little apprehensive as he stepped to the front of the room.

"You've taken my orders the last few months and made the best of them. You haven't argued, haven't fought me and haven't questioned my decisions, you simply understood why I made the choices I made. I want you, and the rest of the pack, to know that I appreciate that, and that it hasn't gone unnoticed. You're reinstated as an Enforcer and I'd like you to take on training some new members into your ranks. August, Vance, Dante, come up here please." I waited for my oldest brother and the two younger Rider males to join us and then smiled at the three of them. "I'd like to welcome the three of you to the ranks of our Enforcers. You'll train with Parker and when he thinks you're ready, you'll take your places as protectors of this pack. Make us proud." The four men beamed up at me as if I had just handed them the keys to the city, each shocked by what they had just heard. "Take your seats." They filed back to their places and I heaved out a heavy breath and gave a nod to open the meeting for questions, several hands went up instantly.

I counted twenty right off and I knew that whatever they had to say, whatever questions they had would only lead to more. This was going to be a long one and I fully expected to be up well past when I normally crawled into bed. I walked around the Alpha's table and settled back into my seat to confer with Frost and our Betas on which questions to take first. Over the last several months we had figured out that some of the older members asked the same questions over and over, regardless of the fact that the response never changed. We finally made a choice and moved back into our places so the circus could begin, a circus that started with Ed, a seventy-four year old who had been a werewolf since he was twenty. He typically had the most valid questions of the elder crowd and whatever answer I gave him would often answer several others as well.

CHAPTER THREE

"WELL THAT was, something." Frost chuckled from her place beside me and then nodded her agreement to my assessment of the meeting we had just concluded. As usual, the same questions had been brought up and the same answers given, again. Between dealing with Freddie and Greg and these meetings, I really was beginning to sound like a broken record. It was getting old, repeating myself over and over again each month. There had been a few new questions, however, all focused around the fact that I had banished a couple of long term pack members to fend for themselves. I was reasonably certain that Greg would be just fine on his own and had actually worried that he might put together a small pack of banished rogues and come back to haunt me later. I couldn't let that color my decision though, I had done what I had to do to make sure that I could lead this pack without too much incident. I leaned back in my chair and let out a heavy sigh as Frost leaned over and rested her head on my shoulder, bringing a smile to my face.

"So what now?" I glanced down at her and took a moment to think it through before I grumbled slightly, knowing what we needed to do.

"Now we wander over to Greg's house and make sure he *actually* cleared out like I told him to. Same with Freddie."

"And if they didn't leave? If they refuse?" I caught her eye as she sat up again and the look I gave her told her everything that she needed to know, I would do whatever I had to do for the pack. "Okay then, let's go get it over with." I gave her a nod and then we both stood and made our way out of the meeting hall and down onto the road. I tugged my jacket tighter around myself and then reached over and looped an arm around my mate's shoulders when I caught the small shiver that rippled through her. We were better in the cold than humans, but we still got cold and since the sun was setting, a rather nasty chill was settling on the area. She leaned into me, her arm finding its way around my waist and her head resting on my shoulder. I didn't have to look down at her to know that her eyes were closed, trusting me to lead the way, to keep her on her feet. I spent the time it took us to walk the distance between the hall and Greg's house to really look around our little piece of the world.

The area had been owned by the Rider pack for generations, claimed before humans settled the area and then purchased legitimately later to make the whole thing legal. The roads were rough, dirt or gravel but kept level and graded by several pack members with the equipment available to smooth them. Most of the original dwellings still existed on the land, older log cabins, hand built ages before most of the current pack was alive. The ones that had been added more recently had a ranch or colonial style to them and while many had been expanded or upgraded, much of the older structures remained. Everything we had as a species, we owned, either having built it with our own hands with the pack's help or purchased outright when we had the funds. The residences; spread out over something like three-hundred and fifty acres, used solar power and rain water reclamation, allowing us to be off the human grid almost completely. These changes had just been put in place in the last decade or so and many packs were making the same adjustments and upgrades. It beat bathing in the streams and lakes and living by lamplight, which some packs still did.

We passed a small strip of shops, nothing big, simple spaces that allowed the pack to make and sell things to the occasional tourist that came through on their way elsewhere. Paintings, handmade furniture and jewelry, breads and cheeses as well as a small bakery and deli, all managed to fit into this small block-and-a-half sized space. Clipper land was a bit closer to human space and so it had a general store and a diner but there was no need for those this far out. The income that these small businesses did bring in typically helped support the pack, as did part of the income of the members who worked outside the pack lands in human settlements. It wasn't that we felt we needed to be apart, we just always had been and back in a time when most of our kind were made by bite or scratch rather than born, this was the safer route. Now we were entering a place where we might not have to settle like this anymore, might not have to hide out in the middle of nowhere.

I thought about that as we walked, wondering how it would feel to live in a human city, to deal with the crowds, the hustle, the traffic, the noise. My nose crinkled a little and I decided that, while I liked visiting, I didn't think I could live that way for any length of time. I had a healthy dose of respect for those of our kind that managed to live in the human world, it couldn't be easy. I scanned the road ahead, smiling into the darkness as a rabbit froze a few yards off the side of the track, sniffed the air, caught our scent and then bounded off into the woods. We might be in human form, but we still smelled like wolves to anything that could tell the difference. Those of our kind that worked with horses and cattle had to work hard at getting the animals to trust them. After all, we smelled like something that should be trying to eat them, not something they wanted riding them or herding them. I grinned at the idea and then returned my gaze to the path ahead of us and took a right when needed.

It was full dark now and the view around us was absolutely beautiful to me, it always had been. We didn't have street lights, there was really no need for them, our kind had superb night vision and could see just fine with a little moon or starlight. This gave everything around us a slightly silver glow as I looked it over, my steps purposeful but not rushed. We had all night if we really wanted to take it, I wasn't about to push myself any faster than necessary tonight. I gave Frost's shoulder a squeeze as we reached Greg's house and she straightened up, opened her eyes and let out a sigh. She had been comfortable right where she had been and while I hated to move her, we had things to do. At first look, things were promising as the lights were all off, the curtains pulled back and I couldn't see any movement inside the house. If we were lucky, he had chosen to leave without putting up any more of a fight, but I knew my luck on these things so I wasn't holding my breath. I took the three small steps up onto his porch and crossed to the door, my mate on my heels, then reached for the knob.

I paused for only a moment before I grabbed it, turned and swung the door open, greeted by the darkness in the space beyond. I scanned the room quickly, clearing it of anything ominous before I stepped in and started through the space. It, thankfully, appeared empty with the personal effects cleared out of the bedroom and bathroom. Upon checking the garage I found Greg's pickup gone as well, the keys to the house left hanging on the wall hook and heaved a huge sigh of relief. He had left without causing any further trouble, thank goodness, now to hope Freddie had done the same. I walked back into the living room where I had left Frost standing and gave her a little wink then nodded for the front door.

"All is clear, let's lock it up and go check Freddie's." We stepped outside, pulling the door closed behind us and I locked it up before we headed out again. When the houses were occupied, we rarely locked the doors; no need to this far out in the middle of nowhere. It was a different story when they were empty; too much of a draw to wandering types looking for a place to stay for the night. Freddie's place was only a bit down the track we'd been walking and as we approached it I frowned, seeing the lights on in the place. Of the two I had expected Greg to put up a fight, not Freddie, I had expected him to run with his tail between his legs just glad to be left alive.

I huffed a little as my brows knit down and Frost glanced from my expression to the house, I felt her tense beside me. "I really hope he just forgot to turn the lights off." I nodded in agreement to that, not interested in getting into it with the older male tonight; he was on thin ice with me as it was. I felt Frost reach over and grab my hand, her fingers slipping between mine seconds before she gave it a supportive squeeze. I looked over, my eyes meeting hers and just gave her a small smile, not saying a word, we were reaching the point where words weren't needed anymore. She winked at me and I just chuckled before giving her hand a return squeeze, dropped it and then took the two stairs up to the porch. I narrowed my eyes as I listened for movement inside for a few seconds then reached up and knocked on the door.

I tilted my head toward the house, listening again and hearing nothing from behind the solid wood door. That was definitely a good sign and I decided to just walk in and take a look around so I reached for the knob. The door was unlocked, not surprising, and I pushed it open completely before I stepped inside. I glanced around the room as Frost stepped in behind me and then ventured further into the house. I found room after room empty and all personal effects removed from the bedroom, glad to find that Freddie had apparently just left the lights on like Frost had suggested.

"Looks good, let's get out of here. I'm ready to go home." Frost nodded at me as I started flipping lights off then she grabbed the keys off the hook near the front door where they had been left and followed me out. Once the place was secure, we returned to our former position, her head on my shoulder and my arm around her so we could walk home. We were about halfway between Freddie's house and our own when I had an idea and just smiled to myself. I started to turn off the road, giving her shoulder a little squeeze so she would know we were taking a detour. She opened her eyes and looked up at me, a question in her eyes and I just smiled and offered her a small shrug in response.

She narrowed her eyes at me but went along with my movement, not really willing to argue with me about it. It was one of the things I loved about her, she trusted me, totally and completely. She was forced to keep her eyes open as we stepped onto a little path between the trees just off the side of the road and headed into the woods. She slipped her hand into my back pocket as we walked and I grinned, feeling the warmth of her skin edging through the denim of my jeans, contrasting with the stark chill of the air around us. I led the way down the trail as it wound its way through the trees, walking on even when the woods grew thicker. We were going somewhere familiar, but coming at it from a different angle than we ever had before and I just grinned, knowing that she would pick up on where we were headed any moment.

I heard her take in a deep breath beside me and knew that she was smelling the same thing I was, the lavender we had planted what felt like ages ago. My gaze worked its way over to her and I caught the smile on her face as she looked over and her eyes met mine. She had it, she knew exactly where we were and the fact that she was grinning like a little kid on Christmas morning made my heart sing. We completed the rest of the walk toward our destination and then slipped from the dense trees into the small glade. It wasn't large enough, or clear enough to be called a clearing, but the canopy was a bit less dense here with one rather large tree taking up most of the space and looking a little out of place. It was a massive willow, its branches sagging in that familiar way; smaller branches creating a wall that didn't conceal as well as it would have with leaves in place.

The branches were long, brushing the ground and even in the middle of the night in the dead of winter I could still see the way it looked in the height of summer. The lavender that usually grew just outside the curtain of branches was mostly dead thanks to the cold, but it was such a strongly scented plant that even this time of year our sensitive noses could still find it. I moved my arm from her waist, sliding my hand down her arm and finding her hand, pulling it from my pocket and slipping my fingers between hers. I turned to face her and walked backwards, leading her into our no longer secret meeting place. It was the first time that we had been back in the glade since we had left for California that night so many months ago. We had been so busy we hadn't managed to slip away and visit it, but tonight seemed perfect for the visit somehow.

CHAPTER FOUR

I stepped under the sparse cover of the leaf-free tree and gave her hand a yank, pulling her against me with a smile. She giggled a little as she slipped her arms around my neck, my own arms finding their way around her waist. I pulled her in closer and kissed her forehead, the contact light and brief, but making her eyes slide closed and pulling a soft sigh from her all the same. The sound made my smile grow and I took the opportunity she'd given me by closing her eyes to trail my lips lightly down the bridge of her nose. I kissed the tip of her nose, making her grin and realized again how much I loved that happy, shy little grin more than I could ever tell her. I brushed my lips across her cheek, down to her chin and then up her jawline to her ear, planting a kiss over the small soft spot just below her ear.

"I love you." I whispered the words softly, just loud enough for her to hear before I moved back down her jawline, catching her lips with mine before she could utter a response. The sharp intake of breath, the sudden meeting of our lips elicited from my mate made my heart flutter a bit. My hands found the hem of her shirt and slipped under it, traveling up over the silky smooth skin of her lower back. I felt her muscles twitch under the feathery touch of my fingertips as they traced ever so lightly across her skin. She sighed against my cheek and leaned in closer against me, the length of her body pressed into mine. My own body reacted instantly, a flush of goose-bumps rushing over me from head to toe as heat gathered between my legs. The chill and the snow were forgotten in that instant, all there was in my senses was Frost and the feel of her against me, in my arms.

When and where she had gained this ability to render my brain a useless mass of blank matter was unknown to me, but I loved it. She was an inch taller than me but that had never mattered, I lifted her off of her feet just as easily as I always had, holding her tight against me as I turned. I walked her over to the massive trunk of the old tree and leaned her back against it as I eased her back down onto her feet, my hands sliding to her hips. Her right knee came up to my hip and I didn't hesitate for even a second before I moved my hand to her thigh just above her knee, holding her leg in place. My right hand slipped back under the hem of her shirt and skimmed along the waistband of her jeans, fingertips brushing from hip to hip. She shivered in my arms and I knew it had nothing to do with the cold. I traced the seam of her lips with the tip of my tongue and she parted them without offering any resistance, allowing my tongue to slide across hers.

She whimpered into the suddenly deepened kiss and a shudder raced through me at the sound, spurring me on. I used my index finger and thumb to flick the button on her jeans open but didn't bother with the zipper; it wouldn't really hinder me as much as the button would anyway. I slipped my fingers below the waistband of her jeans, pressing lower until my fingertips slid over smooth, freshly shaved skin. That forced a low, soft whine to escape my own chest into our kiss which made her pull me closer. I teased over her smooth lips as best as I could manage with her jeans still on and pulled a bit tight thanks to one leg being hiked up to my hip. I knew it managed to be enough when I felt more than heard her moan into my mouth.

Heat flared in my lower body when my fingertip edged just between her already swollen lips and I felt how wet she was. She was more than ready for me, but I wasn't ready to give in and give her what she wanted, what I knew she needed, not just yet. My finger eased up through her wetness slowly, sending a shiver down her body and a whine up from her chest. Ever so slowly my fingertip worked back up until it finally connected with her clit, the first press against the already aroused flesh causing her to break the kiss. "Oh fuck!" I loved it when she cursed, it really only happened when we were like this and that somehow made it endearing. I smiled as she bit her lower lip and opened her eyes to look at me, seeming to finally realize that we were out in the open. Her cheeks flushed a deeper shade of red than they had already been and the look in her eyes said she might be about to stop me.

I wasn't about to let that happen so I leaned into her as my finger started circling the sensitive nub beneath it. She let out a long, low whine and leaned her head down against my neck as her eyes slipped closed again. That was more like it, no fighting; there would be no stopping me when I needed her so badly. Despite the fact that we had only been mated for eight months it had always felt like we had been together forever. Ever since that first night we'd been together like this it was like I had been touching and teasing her for my entire life. I knew what she wanted and I was always prepared to make sure that she got it, and then some. My finger moved slowly at first, a touch and pace that might seem teasing to the point of being mean to some, but that only made her press her hips closer toward me.

Her foot moved around my thigh and she pulled my entire body as close against her as I could possibly get and still be a separate person. After a few moments of the slow pace over her clit, I heard the change in her breathing, the soft hitch from one breath to the next that told me that I was walking the line between pleasing and teasing. I increased the pace and force of the circles, changing direction as well and felt her muscles twitch against me. I could keep this up for only a short time before she would start whining and whimpering at me, but I would do just that. I loved hearing those sounds coming from her and for some reason I needed to hear her beg me tonight. Sure enough, after only a minute or two she let out a somewhat pleading whine at me, telling me she was done with my teasing and wanted more. I normally gave in to the whine, but not this time she would have to tell me what she wanted.

"Kyndle... Please..."

"Please what?" All my answer managed to do was make her whine at me again, not wanting to say it out loud, wanting me to just give in like usual. "Say it, Frost, tell me what you want." I could tell she was weighing the options, pushing me away, whining at me some more or just bucking up and telling me what she wanted. She finally seemed to be giving in as her arms tightened around my shoulders and her lips moved closer to my ear.

"I want you inside me... Fuck me, baby." The words were just the brush of a whisper against my ear, but that was enough, it was all

I needed to hear. I buried my face against the side of her neck as I slid my hand down and pressed two fingers into her, burying them all the way inside her heated, arousal-slicked core in one move. She tensed in my arms, a gasp ripping from her lips as her nails dug into my back through my shirt and I felt her teeth graze my skin. I gave her a moment to adjust to the sensation and then I eased my fingers back out slowly before thrusting them back in completely. I quickly picked up a pace that I knew would drive her over the edge fast, normally liking drawing our encounters out but not particularly wanting to get caught. While I was Alpha, it would still be awkward to be caught by any of our younger pack members fucking my mate against a tree out in the middle of the woods.

I kept up my pace, pushing into her fast and deep, listening as her ragged panting turned into pleading little moans in my ear. Her hips moved with my hand, meeting each of my thrusts in perfect time, forcing me as deep as I could possibly go. She released a string of breathy expletives against my neck and I smiled as I decided to be a little mean. I felt her muscles twitch around my fingers, my cue if I was going to do what I was thinking. I pulled out of her completely, ripping a pathetic-sounding whimper from her lips as she moved one hand to reach for my arm. I took my hand from her leg to brush her hand away from my arm, keeping her from interfering. "Kyndle... Don't do this. Please baby... Please..." The sound of her whining at me broke me down and I grabbed her leg again, slid my hand back down and wasted no time in pushing my fingers back into her, the original two now replaced with three, curled just so, hitting that spot inside I knew she loved so much.

That was all it took to make her come undone and she dragged her nails down the back of my shirt as she threw her head back against the tree trunk and screamed my name. I leaned in and gripped the soft flesh at the base of her neck between my teeth as my thumb grazed over her clit, pushing her further into her climax. I sucked on her neck as she tightened around my fingers harder, riding out the waves of her peak as they crashed over her. Her muscles eventually started to relax and she leaned against me, allowing me to support her weight as she rode the little ripple of aftershocks that coursed through her for a few minutes. I broke the lock I had on her neck and nuzzled the already-darkening area, a small, very canine sounding purr edging out against her skin.

She held onto me like her life depended on it, her breathing still shallow and ragged, her eyes closed and her fingers now tangled in my hair. Once I felt her pulse begin to steady and her breathing becoming regular again, I released her leg, letting her foot ease back to the ground as I placed a few light kisses up her neck.

"I love you." I smiled as the whispered words reached my ears and wrapped my arms around her waist, hugging her tight.

"I love you, too, Frost." I felt her smile against my neck as I moved to kiss her temple and then I leaned back a little, reaching up to catch her chin between the thumb and index finger of my right hand so I could make her look at me. "Come on my love, let's go home." She nodded a little then let me take a step back before she took my hand and we took one last look around our spot before heading out. We had been coming to the place since we were just over fifteen, but had never connected within it the way that we just had. As special as the small glade had been before, after tonight it would always hold an extra special place, for the both of us, I knew that much without even having to ask her.

We made our way back to the road, neither of us speaking, not feeling the need to fill the stillness of the night with chatter. The sounds of the winter woods surrounded us, a deer off in the distance pawing through the snow looking for food, a bear snoring softly in its den nearby, an owl hooting off to our left. It was all so perfect and I was eternally grateful that I would get to continue to experience it all with Frost at my side. We made it back to the house and stepped through our front door, shedding our coats and hanging them on the rack to the left of the entryway. I moved into the living room to start a fire as Frost headed for the kitchen to make some tea for us. By the time I had the fire going and the space was warming and filled with the crackling and flickers of red, orange and yellow, Frost was back and setting two mugs of steaming tea on the coffee table.

I stood from where I had been squatting by the fireplace and nudged the logs around a little with the poker, making sure they weren't going to fall out and burn the house down. I had just returned the tool to its place on the rack when I felt warm arms circle my waist, tugging my lips up into a smile. Frost leaned against my back and brushed her lips up my neck, the touch just ghosting across my skin. I shivered at the contact as she reached my ear, tightened her arms around me and nipped at me earlobe. "My turn." Those two whispered words dropped the smile right off my face as she eased one hand down the front of my jeans, making my eyes go wide and kicking my pulse into overdrive.

Chapter Five

THE SUN streaming through the gap in the living room curtains and falling across my face pulled me from my sleep. I stretched, felt Frost's arm tighten around my waist, her naked body pressed against my back and smiled as the previous night filtered back into my mind. We hadn't even made it into the bedroom after she had pinned me in front of the fireplace in the living room. We had just pulled the throw pillows and blankets from the couch seat and spent the night enjoying each other right there in front of the fire. I took a deep breath and then let out a slow, contented sigh as I snuggled back against my mate, linking my fingers with hers and pulling her hand up so I could kiss her knuckles.

She rewarded my gentle kiss with a soft purr against the back of my neck and a few much enjoyed nuzzles. We lay like that for several minutes, not caring that we had things to do and should probably get up and get the day started. I finally had no choice but to get up, my body insisting that I needed a trip to the bathroom and probably some food so I grumbled a little, extracted myself from Frost's arms and padded down the hallway. I returned a few minutes later to find that she hadn't moved a bit while I had been away other than to drag the pillow I had been using into her arms so she was now cuddling it in my absence. I let out a little chuckle as I crossed the room, sat down behind her and leaned over to brush my lips across her ear.

"Should I be jealous of my own pillow?" She grinned at my comment as she turned onto her back and stretched, easing her eyes open to look up at me. As always, those purple orbs meeting mine made my heart flutter in my chest, I loved that feeling so much.

"Mmm, depends, are you planning on coming back or do I need to keep snuggling this pillow?"

"Sorry love, up for the day. You should be too, come on."

My reply had a bit of a laugh behind it as I shook my head and reached out to give a few stray strands of her hair a light tug. She grumbled, faked a frown at me and pulled the pillow she'd been cuddling over her face to block the room out.

"Oh come on you, up."

She shook her head under the pillow, throwing an arm across it to keep it in place, showing no signs of moving. I raised an eyebrow at her as my eyes trailed down her upper body, exposed to the morning light when she had turned over. I reached over and brushed my fingertips down her bare stomach, just barely grazing her skin and making a flush of goose-bumps break out across her body. She swatted at my hand and then hit me in the shoulder with the pillow that had been covering her face as I laughed.

"Would you cut it out, you brat? Didn't you get enough last night?" I smirked at her as she looked up at me then yanked the pillow out of her hands and leaned down to press a quick kiss to her lips.

"Get enough of you moaning in my ear and screaming my name? Never gonna happen, gorgeous." I waggled my eyebrows at her suggestively and she rolled her eyes and shoved me away so she could sit up.

"Pervert."

"You know it." Another eye roll from her accompanied my laugh as she pushed herself off the floor, stretched her arms up over her head and then headed upstairs to get ready. I just sat there, watching her walk away, one eyebrow lofting slightly while my eyes followed the sway of her hips as she ascended the stairs.

"Stop staring at my ass, perv."

I laughed, not even trying to deny that I'd been doing just that, pushed myself off the floor and started up after her. Once we were showered, dried and dressed for the day, we returned to the living room to put it back together, returning the blankets and pillows to their places. One last look around the room to make sure everything was in its place and we headed for the kitchen, our stomachs finally winning out. She settled in making coffee as I started cooking breakfast, grumbling as I managed to spill raw egg on my long sleeved tee. Frost giggled and handed me a wet rag so I could clean it up, earning her a quick kiss for the gesture.

Once everything was finished, we loaded it onto plates, filled our mugs with freshly brewed caffeinated goodness and settled in at the table. We chatted while we ate, lingering at the table for several minutes after our plates were empty to finish our coffee. Once that was gone we couldn't justify sitting there any longer so we gathered our dishes, loaded them into the dishwasher and started gathering the things we would need for the day. Pockets loaded and jackets pulled on, we headed out, locking the front door before we started for the car sitting out front. I stopped dead in my tracks when I saw my father leaning against the passenger door of the vehicle, arms crossed over his chest and a glare leveled at me.

My brother Brandon was sitting on the hood, one booted foot up on the bumper, but he refused to look at me. I looked between the two men a couple times then allowed my gaze to settle on my father, trying to keep the glare off my face.

"What do you want, Dane?"

I watched as his glare took on a hard edge when I used his first name, the ultimate disrespect from one of his children in his book. The question also made Brandon's head snap up and his gaze center on me finally, the expression on his face a mix of shock and what looked a little like pride in my gutsy wording. I clipped my keys to my pocket and hooked my thumbs in my belt loops, adopting a much more easygoing stance than my father, something that he noticed. He pushed off the car, standing up to his full height and dropped his arms, his hands finding his pockets as he looked at me.

"I think you meant 'What do you want, sir?' or maybe 'father' or even 'Alpha'?"

"Nope. None of the above. I meant what I said. I no longer feel that father fits. I don't want that tie to you. Sir and Alpha? I don't think so, you aren't my Alpha anymore, never will be again."

I watched the anger flare behind his eyes, but I didn't flinch or really react to it at all other than letting the left corner of my lips twitch slightly, the beginning of a grin that I caught and managed to hold back.

"I've been waiting, hoping that you would forget this ridiculous idea of leading a pack and take a step back. Apparently, you're still just as stubborn as you always were growing up. Since you refuse to see reason, I'm left with no alternative. The challenge happens tonight, be ready."

I just nodded then watched as he and Brandon moved back toward the truck and then made their way off of our property and back to Clipper land. My expression was schooled, calm, but my stomach was twisting itself into a knot and my pulse was racing. Frost could sense how panicked I really was and eased her arms around my waist, resting her chin on my shoulder gently.

"Relax sweetheart. It'll be okay, you can do this."

I felt a fraction better knowing that she believed in me, I just wished that I could believe in me as fervently. I let out a sigh and leaned back against her, closing my eyes and taking a moment to let the tension ease out of my shoulders and back. Dane had always made me tense, I just hadn't realized how bad it was until I didn't live under his roof and actually had mostly tension-free days. I managed to smile when Frost nuzzled my neck and instantly felt the knot that had been rapidly forming between my shoulders loosen and fade. How she managed to relax me so completely without doing much of anything would always amaze and confuse me, but I was thankful for it. I turned my head slightly so I could press a light kiss to her lips and then leaned away and reluctantly removed myself from her embrace.

"We should get moving, if I have to manage a fight to the death tonight we have a lot to do first." My tone was teasing, but I knew by the look in her eyes that Frost knew I was worried. She could read me like a book, just like I could with her. "Honestly, baby, I'm as alright as I'm gonna be. Let's just get through today and then deal with tonight when we get to it."

She offered me a slow nod in response, but I could tell that she just wanted to cancel whatever we needed to get done, go back inside and spend the day wrapped up together. I gave a little nod toward the car and she finally moved toward it, sliding into the passenger seat when I opened her door for her. I leaned down, used a finger to turn her face toward me and kissed her, lingering a moment before I pulled back and closed the door. Once I was around the car and settled in, I started it up and headed out for our first stop of the day. We'd had a plan that we would be sticking with, but I would be tacking on one extra stop at the end, Abbey and Kyle's house. I needed to tell them what had taken place and make sure they would be there when this fight happened.

Our first item on the daily agenda was to meet with the

cleaning and remodel crew at Greg's old house to do a walk-through. We were having the two recently vacated houses cleaned top to bottom and then having the wiring, plumbing and flooring updated in them. It had been ages since either had been cleaned up properly and they were in dire need of a visit from some pine-sol or maybe just straight bleach. Once we had walked through Greg's old place and gone over the list on it, we met the second crew at Freddie's old place and did the same with them.

That task completed, we made our way into Billings for a standing lunch date with Abbey's parents and the third in line of my four brothers, Tristan. He hadn't rebelled enough to leave the pack like Dante and Shane had, but he completely refused to cut me out of his life. I was thankful for that, more than I honestly ever thought I'd be able to tell him. Normally Abbey and Kyle would join us for lunch, but Kyle's parents were passing through town and had requested lunch with the two of them. They would be meeting Abbey's parents over dinner that night, I hoped the two couples would get along, for my best friend's sake.

We met Austin and Becca outside the small café then walked in together, being led back and seated in a booth almost immediately.

"Okay girl. Spill it. What's going on?"

I feigned a confused look in Austin's direction, one eyebrow arced up as if asking him what he was talking about.

"Nice try, but I'm not buying it. Kyndle, you've been like a second child to us for years, we know you better than that, sweetheart. Talk."

I let out an exasperated huff and rolled my eyes, having known deep down that I wouldn't be able to hide my inner tension from Austin. He could pinpoint my tension almost as well as Abbey and Frost could, disconcerting to say the least to have people know you that well, but nice at the same time.

"Fine. Dane showed up in front of our house this morning. He's following through with the challenge... Tonight."

I saw Rebecca's eyes go wide in my peripheral vision at the same time that Austin's fell into a glare.

"Are you kidding me?" I pursed my lips and shook my head, I only wished he was kidding, that he would show up and tell me he was joking then we'd laugh it off. That wasn't Dane though, he didn't joke, he didn't kid and he was more pissed at me right now than anyone really realized. "Well damn. What can we do? Any way we can help, we will. I know he's my Alpha but he's pushing the limits of that title, as well as the friend one he's barely holding on to."

"Nothing you really can do, Austin. Just be here, support me in this."

He nodded his agreement then turned to Rebecca and took a deep breath as their eyes met, a question passing wordlessly between them.

"We're there, and we'll stay there. I'm finished with his tirades, this was the last straw. Becca and I discussed what we would do if he went through with this ordeal and we agreed. If he insisted on following through with his challenge we were leaving, since it appears he has decided to push this issue, we're through."

CHAPTER SIX

I WAS shocked at what I was hearing from Austin, despite the fact that I had asked him to do just what he was suggesting, defect from the Clippers, a few short months ago, it was still a shock. He had been loyal to my father for longer than even my oldest brother had been alive and turning his back on that was huge. It was a major step for a Beta to turn on his Alpha and walk away from his pack, a hard step and I could tell that despite his determination, he was hurting over the choice.

"Thank you, both of you. I know this isn't easy, and it won't be easy but... I don't intend to lose this challenge."

"We know."

I just offered a slow nod to his short reply, knowing that he understood that if one of us had to die, I had no intention of it being me, which meant my father would fall. We managed to bring the conversation to something less life-ending and chatted as we ordered and then ate. It was a pleasant distraction from what I was heading into that night and I was glad for it. Once we finished and Austin and I argued over who would be picking up the tab, an argument I was happy to win, we said our goodbyes and went our separate ways. Austin and Rebecca had agreed to be at the fight that night and regardless of the outcome would not be returning to Clipper land afterward.

The news was a bit sobering as I realized that there was a very real chance that my best friend, her mate, her parents and more importantly, my mate, could end up with no place to call home by the end of the night. I was silent as we made our way back toward pack land to meet up with Abbey and Kyle and Frost left me to my thoughts for the duration of the drive.

"Baby, what's on your mind? Talk to me."

I had just parked the car and she had apparently decided she was done keeping quiet and letting me torment myself. I glanced over at her, the hurt over what had been running through my mind plain in my eyes as they held hers.

"If I lose..."

"Don't, Kyndle. Don't go there."

She may have cut me off, but I needed to say what I was thinking, it needed out and I waved her off with a shake of my head so I could continue.

"I'm serious, Frost. If I lose... Run. Get as far away from this place as you can. If he gets through me, you'll be next and I can't even think about..." I got choked up and had to stop and take a deep, ragged breath to steady my nerves and my twisting stomach. "I can't even think about him hurting you. Just get away from here, as far and as fast as you can. I have to know that if anything happens to me, you'll be safe, you'll be alive." She stared back at me, her eyes locked on mine as I watched them mist over, her chin quivering with the effort of holding the tears back.

"Alive? What good is being alive if I don't have you?"

My stomach knotted tightly and I swear that my heart died a little at the pain in her voice as she spoke the words. I reached over as tears began to fall down her left cheek and used my thumb to brush them away.

"Baby, don't cry. Look, I don't plan on losing this thing. I just prefer to be prepared for the worst, okay?" She sniffed as she gave me a small nod and I reached down, hit the lever to push my seat all the way back and then grabbed her hand and gave it a tug. "Come here sweetheart." She crawled over the console between the seats and curled herself onto my lap, her head on my shoulder and her arms around my waist. I wrapped one arm around her shoulders, the other running through her pale hair as I rocked her slightly. "We'll get through this."

She nodded against my shoulder, but her tears didn't stop, and I didn't try and talk her down from the crying. She needed this, needed to get it out, to worry about me and I wasn't about to tell her she couldn't. As much faith as she had in me and my ability to win this thing, she was still terrified she was going to lose me deep down in the darkness.

I sat there for a little over half an hour, holding her, letting her cry and doing my best to not start doing the same. The last thing she needed was for me to fall apart too, that wouldn't help anything so I held it together, for her. We sat there long enough that Abbey came out to make sure we were okay, but when she saw Frost curled up in my lap, she gave me a sad smile, nodded when I returned it and then went back inside to wait for us. I didn't know how long she would need to get herself together, but I would sit and hold her for as long as it took.

She slowly stopped crying, her sniffles becoming fewer and farther between until she was silent in my embrace. The knot in my stomach had tightened and my heart hurt knowing how upset this whole ordeal had made my mate. I was determined to win this challenge, I couldn't leave her, not if this was the preview of what she would go through without me. She finally leaned away from me, giving a last sniffle and then pressing her lips to mine. The kiss was slow and deep, but not as frantic or passion-filled as usual. It was a reassurance, a way for her to remind herself that I was still right here and that I loved her.

She pulled away after a couple minutes and I brushed a few stray strands of her hair behind her ear with a small smile. "Try not to worry about it. What's meant to be, shall be." She managed a sad little smile and a nod then sighed and leaned her forehead against mine. "Come on, let's go in, they're waiting for us."

She kissed the tip of my nose and then reached over and popped my door open so she could slide out of the car. I readjusted my seat and then slipped out as well, taking her hand as I shut the door. We walked to up the lawn and across the porch together, Abbey tugging the door open before we'd even had the chance to knock on it. She pulled Frost into a hug, holding her for a minute as my mate hugged her back and I mouthed a 'thank you' at her for the comforting gesture. She finally released my mate and then reached over and pulled me into a tight hug, one that I couldn't help but return. The hugs were followed by hugs from Kyle as well and I had the feeling that Austin had already called and told Abbey what was going on.

We all finally settled in the living room and I let out a heavy sigh as Frost cuddled in close against my side then I wrapped an arm around her. "Dad called." I just nodded at my best friend as she confirmed what I'd already known. I honestly didn't mind. It meant that I didn't have to go over all of it again. I would just have to answer a couple questions. "I can't believe he's going through with this. It's ridiculous, he's your father!" I just shrugged, what could I really say to that statement that would make any sense to anyone. "What is he thinking? I mean, is he so against you leading a pack of your own that he would risk having to... To... Well you know, just to take it away from you?"

I couldn't blame her for not saying the word, for being unable to put it out there and give it weight and voice. Risk having to kill me, kill his own daughter, and I just took a deep breath, exhaled slowly and nodded at her.

"He would, and he's going too. He doesn't care, Abbey. I don't think he ever really did. I never felt like he loved any of us. We were just more pack members he could boss around and rule over, that's all. Deep down I think he might even hate me a little." She scoffed at that, apparently unable to believe that my own father, the man who had helped give me life, could hate me enough to want to take that very life away. I felt Frost shiver beside me and I pulled her tighter against my side as she leaned her head on my shoulder. This was wearing on her and I was glad that it would be over in a few short hours, though I was praying that it would have the outcome we all wanted. "Look, I just need you there, both of you. I know you can't jump in and help me or anything, but I need all the support I can get tonight."

"Oh we'll be there, don't worry about that. We have faith in you, Kyndle. If anyone can come out the other side of this shit-storm, it's you, girl." I gave Kyle the best smile I could manage, which I knew still looked strained and a little sad, but it was all I had in me. Abbey nodded her agreement to his words and then reached over and got hold of my free hand, giving it a squeeze.

"Thanks guys, that means a lot to me. I just want this to be over with already."

Everyone nodded their agreement to that and then we changed the subject, chatting about anything else that came to mind. Abbey and I regaled Frost and Kyle with stories of the trouble we had gotten into when we were younger and we all actually managed to have a few chuckles. Evening rolled around and there was a knock at the door, Abbey had told us that she had invited her parents over to have dinner with us since Kyle's parents had to leave and head back to California early. It was a good idea, it gave them a reason to be coming to our pack land before the fight so that they were here when it began. She answered the door and then led them into the living room so they could join us. Kyle had excused himself to the back patio to get the grill going and the scent of burning charcoal wafted through the house. Greetings were exchanged as they took their seats and then Abbey brought everyone a fresh round of soda and coffee and we all chatted lightly until the food was ready.

Dinner was a quiet and rather somber affair with very little conversation taking place around the table. I ate what I could, but ended up just pushing most of the food around my plate in a daze, barely seeing it and not hearing any of the small talk going on around me. I had pulled back into my head, trying to get myself in the right mindset for what would be taking place in the next couple hours. I was still a bit nervous about the whole thing, but I was honestly more scared than anything, even though it killed me to admit it. My blood was running cold and I was chilled straight through despite the warmth inside Abbey's house.

I was so lost in thought that I jumped when I felt fingertips brush my cheek and then turned a sheepish smile on Frost as she tucked some hair behind my ear. She didn't speak, she didn't need to say anything as she hooked the back of my neck with her hand, pulled me over and kissed my forehead. I sucked in a ragged sounding breath and sat there, eyes closed, hand finding her forearm and holding on as she brushed her thumb over the side of my neck.

I finally opened my eyes and looked at her, our eyes meeting across the small space between our chairs and what I saw reflected in hers made my heart soar. This amazing, intense, beautiful woman sitting beside me loved me, so much that I could see the fire burning in her eyes. She believed in me, despite the fear of losing me, she had faith that I could make it through this, that I wouldn't leave her.

"We'll meet you guys in the clearing later. I think Frost and I need some time alone."

Four nods from the other occupants of the table was the response to my words and that was all I needed. I took my mate's hands, stood from the chair I was in and then pulled her to her feet in front of me. I led her to the door, helped her into her jacket and then slipped into mine before we stepped out into the chilled December night. I took her hand as we reached the road, slipping my fingers between hers to link them together and then brought them up, kissing her knuckles lightly.

"I hate this, Kyn. Why can't everyone just leave us alone? Let us be?"

I didn't have an answer for her because I had been asking myself that same thing for a while now, never getting an answer to it myself.

"It won't get any easier anytime soon. You know if..." I caught myself, I couldn't think 'if', I wouldn't. If I let that doubt squeeze its way into my head it would make itself at home and just trip me up. "When I win this, the Elders will have something to say about it for sure. That council is full of men that were friends with my father before they became Elders and that doesn't lean in our favor, regardless of the outcome of this fight."

She gave a small nod and then looked up into the sky, the light covering of clouds over head glowed faintly in the last remaining rays of light emanating from the tiny sliver of waning moon out. I kept walking, leading the way to a small picnic area about a quarter mile from Abbey and Kyle's house. I stepped into the space, her hand still held tightly in mine and then gave it a tug, pulling her over to me. I turned her so her back was against my chest, my arm around her waist, hands still linked as my other arm slid around her.

"This all feels so, I don't know, like a bad dream I can't wake up from. I just wish they'd all let us live our lives."

Her voice was small, like she was afraid that speaking any louder would just bring more terrible luck down on us.

"I know, honey, but you know they won't, they don't know how. They aren't happy unless they're judging someone and we're easy to judge." She nodded a little, knowing it was true, as diverse and misunderstood a group as our species was, we could be damn quick to judge. Those in the generations before ours were completely against what we represented, in more than one way. We were young, not even out of our teens, we were female, a major strike against us in the eyes of an older, completely male council, and to top it off we were queer.

Forgetting the other things that would irritate them, being lesbians made them hate us on principle, they didn't want our kind even in the packs, much less leading them. I had often caught myself wondering over the last few months how Barkley and Hank managed to keep their pack together. The only conclusion I could come up with was that they flew under the radar, kept a low profile.

Despite being a large pack they were settled, happy and the council had no reason to look more closely at them, or their relationship. We didn't have that luxury, we had been under their scrutiny since day one and had already heard that at least three of the five council members were tucked away on Clipper land, waiting.

"They're just looking for reasons to run us off, aren't they?"

All I could do was nod against her shoulder, as terrible as it sounded, it was true, they wanted us gone and they would find a way. I had to wonder if they would use the outcome of this challenge to force us out. It was a very real possibility. The thought of having to leave and resettle was a little terrifying if I was being honest, but it was something we might very well have to deal with. I closed my eyes and turned my face into Frost's neck, breathing in her scent, letting it surround me and ease my rapidly fraying nerves. Her scent had shifted slightly since we had bonded, as I knew mine had also and I let the mingled tendrils of snow, willow and lavender wrap around me. I loved her scent, it was comforting to every one of my senses, it smelled like home and I knew it always would.

"Come on, time to get this circus started."

She let out a soft whine, but a moment later I felt the bob of her head as she nodded and then loosened my grip as she turned in my arms, dropping my hand so she could ease her palms up onto my cheeks. We stood there for a moment, gazes locked as those intense purple orbs stared right into my very soul. She leaned in and pressed her lips to mine and I felt the urgency behind her kiss, hoping that it wouldn't be our last, but putting everything she felt for me behind it just in case it was. When we parted, both a little breathless, I actually managed to smile at her and she offered me one in return. No words were spoken as we linked hands and started toward the clearing the challenge would take place in. It was time to meet my future, I just hoped that it was one that we would be able to live with, live in.

CHAPTER SEVEN

NEWS OF the challenge had spread quickly and by the time we entered the clearing there was a crowd gathered. I scanned the faces I could see, knowing that the majority of them were here hoping I would lose, that my father would take my place and take over the Rider pack and they wanted to see it firsthand. It was a heart-wrenching thought, but I tried not to dwell on it for too long, it would just be a distraction. I turned my attention to the clear spot behind me when I heard footfalls and managed a small smile at Abbey, Kyle, Austin and Rebecca. Shane and Dante were with them and the sight of the six of them standing there with Frost was enough to bolster my nerves.

I had support and that was all that mattered in the few minutes that were to follow, that this group believed in me. They were my family, not all by blood, but every one of them by something much stronger, love, and that meant more. I took a deep breath as I exchanged glances with each of them, finally ending with my eyes locked on Frost's. A sudden calm washed over me and I knew that I could handle this, as well as whatever was to follow, as long as she was by my side. I gave her a small nod, which she returned, and then turned toward the sounds of murmurs and chatter rippling through the group present.

Dane had arrived with Brandon and Tristan in tow and I was shocked to see my mother standing between my two brothers. The fact that he had made her come to this display, this horrific match up where either her mate or her only daughter would end up dead, was sickening. He was more twisted than I had ever realized and suddenly my motivation to win had an entirely new level. I had to get my mother out from under his stranglehold, away from his tyranny and hope she could still recover. With any luck at least one of my remaining brothers would leave the old pack and join us.

I watched as my father turned and addressed some of the Clipper members nearest him, not caring what he was saying enough to try and hear it. I waited for him to finish speaking and then cocked my head at him slightly when he turned around to face me. His glare cut right through me, but I kept any sign of that off my face, my expression a carefully schooled mask that showed nothing but calm. That seemed to irritate him and his neck flushed red, his eyes darkening as he readied himself to shift forms. I did the same, dropping clothes to the ground without losing eye contact, intent on staring him down at the very least.

I stood stock still as he shifted, watching with a bit of curiosity as the shift took him several long seconds and almost seemed painful. Thinking back, he had always had difficulty shifting and I had to wonder now if he and his wolf were ever on the same page about things. Typically when the two halves were in balance the shift was quick, easy and flawless, like mine had become, like Frost's always had been. This made for an interesting bit of information that I hadn't counted on. Being out of balance with half of his own being would make him overly reactive and easy to push into making mistakes.

I smirked as his shift finally completed and I heard him growl at me across the clearing, clearly angry that I had found anything to even begin to smile about. He launched at me and I simply cocked my head back the other way a bit and watched him come at me. I wasn't feeling particularly cocky, I just knew that my shift was quick and that processing his movements in human form would be a more thorough endeavor. He drew close enough to leap at me, but the moment his paws left the ground I dropped to my hip, sliding under him and shifting before he had even landed. When he turned on me, he seemed a bit out of sorts with the fact that my wolf was facing him rather than my human form.

I barked at him, not a happy sound, instead something holding a tense warning, telling him that I was prepared to do whatever I had to do to walk away from this encounter. He growled in response and then lowered his head, ears pinned against his neck, lips pulled back in a snarl that showed his canines clearly. I had to admit that he was a bit terrifying, standing there across from me, dwarfing my wolf by at least six inches and still looking healthy and fit despite the white and silver salting his otherwise dark charcoal pelt. That feeling caused me to grumble at myself, I wasn't about to let my old fear of him taint my confidence.

I huffed, more at myself than him and rather than cower like the good little girl he wanted and expected me to be, I pulled myself up a little taller. My ears perked forward, paws set firm in the dirt and tail held high, the stance of an Alpha showing her dominance. That had exactly the effect I'd been hoping for. It pissed him off and he snarled a split second before he launched at me again, determined to end this quickly. I had no intention of letting this end quickly, I was younger and had better stamina than he did, I could play at this a lot longer than he could. I planned to work that to my advantage and wear him down slowly, run out his energy and make him rethink this whole idea.

With any luck I could get him to admit defeat and give in without having to end the night in too much bloodshed. I sidestepped as he reached me then threw my entire weight against his side as he passed me, sending him sprawling sideways in the dirt. He was back on his feet a moment later, his gaze on me and when I saw his eyes, they were a startling onyx that I'd never seen before. He was so full of anger, of rage and of hatred that I didn't even think he knew what he was angry at anymore. His life seemed to be one endless circle of anger, disappointment and hate that he didn't even bother to try and dig out of, at least, not anymore.

I wondered how long it had been eating away at him, how long he had been carrying so much negative energy inside himself. I shook the thought off, not really wanting to start feeling bad for him when that would only make me hesitate. I couldn't afford to miss even a single step tonight, not if I wanted to walk away from this. There wasn't a choice there, I had to walk away from this. My vision narrowed down as he lowered himself just a bit, preparing to launch at me again and the rest of the clearing slipped away. It was just the two of us now, no one else existed, and nothing else mattered in that moment, just defeating him and staying alive.

He moved, I reacted, faking a duck that threw him off just a bit, enough for me to catch the side of his neck and jerk at the skin with enough force to slam him to the ground. I released him from my grip and instantly regretted it as his jaws closed around my right front leg. I yelped then just barely managed to yank the appendage from his teeth before he could clamp down and break my leg. I was bleeding, but the leg was still usable and could bear weight, that was all that mattered in the moment. The move left me determined to keep on my toes, not wanting him to get another blow in since I might not be as lucky the next time.

I knew that I needed to land a few decent blows, something that would disable him without killing him. I knew he was out to kill me, and I would end his life if I had no choice, but I preferred not to if I could help it. I stared him down, my blood staining the white patch of fur on his chin crimson and the sight made my stomach flutter. My father, the man who had helped give me life, was determined enough to be the one that ended it that he had my blood on his mouth. The thought was simultaneously terrifying and sobering and I took in a sharp breath then exhaled heavily.

I finally realized that he might just make it impossible for me to let him live, something that I hadn't counted on, but should have. We stood there for what felt like an eternity, staring each other down, seconds ticking by as we seemed to reevaluate each other. His next movement was sudden and startled me slightly, but I recovered quickly enough to drop flat to the ground so that he couldn't reach my throat. His teeth sank into my scruff, tearing at the skin and making me launch to my feet and twist to get out of his grip. I got free and took several steps back, only to be met with his smug face watching the blood stain the fur on my shoulder as it flowed.

The self-righteous bastard was actually enjoying this and that was sicker than I could really handle so I shoved the idea out of my mind. I was done playing nice, done sparing him and attempting to run him down since he was obviously trying to end my life. My head dropped, the fur down my back bristling up as I loosed a deep growl at him, ready for his next move. This time, when he moved, I was only a split second behind the action and moved right with him. The feel of my teeth ripping into flesh followed by the sound of my fathers' yelp of pain was enough to tell me I had hit my mark.

I released his back leg quickly and jerked back before he could turn on me and wound me yet again, I couldn't afford any further injury. I hadn't taken the leg out, but I had done some damage and managed to stay clear of his jaws as they snapped closed on the empty space I had occupied only moments before. His eyes flashed at me, red beginning to rim the black that they had turned earlier and showing the rage that was filling him. My own ice blue irises met those hate-filled orbs and a new thought hit me in that moment, one that tipped the scales. My father was weak.

He had allowed anger, hurt, rage and hatred to take over his being and it was crippling him in a way he couldn't even see. He had always seemed so untouchable, so much larger than life and so he had been scary to my younger self. He had terrified me for as long as I could remember, but now suddenly he just didn't anymore. Even as I stood there bleeding from the bites he had left behind on my wolf form, I no longer feared him. The simple yet profound epiphany turned the tables and changed everything in ways that no one could actually see as they watched us.

My pulse slowed, my mind drew back from the frantic pace it had been working at and eased into a steady focus, my breathing evened out and I felt a calmness wash over me that I hadn't thought possible. Dane was unaware of the changes that had just taken place in me, though his wolf should have been able to detect the shift in my breathing and heart rate, he was too far gone already. He moved again, barreling down on me and rather than move, rather than sidestep or dodge him, I squared the set of my canine shoulders and leaned forward as he slammed into me.

I was ready when his head connected with my chest and I took the force of the hit, feeling my body pushed back a few feet, my paws sliding through the dirt. I felt a snap, knowing instantly that when I shifted back my collarbone would more than likely be broken, but I stayed upright. Once the movement stopped, I grabbed the back of his neck in my jaws, shocking him enough to render him motionless for a second. In that moment I shifted to my left, my side coming flush against his body, and pressed my shoulder down into the top of his, forcing him down to the ground. My jaws tightened down, making sure that he knew it wasn't just skin I had between my teeth, but muscle and bone as well.

A few more pounds of pressure and it would all be over, he would be removed from the equation and I would walk away from this ordeal. I growled down at him and he let out a whimper, sounding more pitiful than I had ever heard him sound in all my eighteen years of life. I paused for a moment, considering the options, wondering if it was possible to let him live and still have him out of my way. He felt my hesitation and started to move, my reaction time just a fraction better than he had bargained for as I pinned him right back down. He snarled at me and in that moment,

I had my answer, he had told me everything that I needed to know in a single, simple action.

I closed my eyes, steeling myself against what I was about to do and then inhaled slowly, filling my lungs to capacity. I held the breath for a moment, willed myself to do what had to be done and as I exhaled I clamped my jaws down hard. The tearing of muscle and tendons and snapping of bones wasn't nearly as easy on my already battered mental state as Cameron's had been. I held on, not daring to release him until I knew it was over as my senses began to return to normal. My hearing returned and the silence that had settled around me let me know that it was over, it was finished. I released my grip and heard the thump of dead weight hitting the dirt, but refused to look down.

Despite what he had put me through, I wasn't sure I could handle seeing my father's lifeless body at my feet. I had done what needed to be done, but that didn't mean that I had to like it, or that I had to revel in it. I wouldn't be rejoicing in this victory, not when the cost had been so high. Regardless of how he had treated me, in spite of the pain he had put me through for so many years, it was still his blood running through my veins and I wasn't ready to face the fact that his death was on my hands.

CHAPTER EIGHT

I TURNED away from the body I still wouldn't look at and padded back over to where I had left my clothes. I shifted back, dressed and then stood there, staring at the ground between my still bare feet, numb. I felt arms slip around me from behind and closed my eyes as the familiar scent of my mate enveloped me in a loving warmth I hadn't even realized I needed. My chin dropped to my chest and I let out a ragged sigh before I forced myself to open my eyes, turn around and look at her. She moved one hand to brush my hair from my face and then let her palm settle against my cheek lightly.

Neither of us spoke, we just stood there, eyes locked as the world faded away for a few much needed moments. Reality would set back in shortly and I needed to escape it for as long as possible before dealing with the inevitable fallout. I felt her squeeze my hip and took the gesture for what it was meant to be, a small show of support in me, in my choice. I shifted my gaze over her shoulder when I heard someone clear their throat and caught sight of my mother standing there watching us. My brows knit together as she approached, not sure what was about to happen and not completely convinced that she wouldn't be livid with me for what I had done.

My father had made her life a living hell for the last three decades or so, but that didn't mean she'd wanted him gone forever. As she closed in on where we were standing, I moved Frost so she was standing behind me and met my mother's gaze. I was stunned for a moment when she wrapped her arms around me and buried her head against my shoulder. I felt Frost move and glanced over at her, catching the small smile that had taken over her features. I turned my eyes toward my mother where she was hugging me, then back to my mate and then finally managed to smile a little. Apparently, she wasn't as mad as I had feared she would be for what I had done, but I had to know what she was thinking.

"Mom, are you okay?"

At first, she just nodded against my shoulder, but then she leaned away from me and took a shaky breath.

"I'm alright. It was a horrible spot to be in, but I'm glad it was you that won."

I went a little wide eyed at that since I had spent the last several years just assuming that my mother didn't care about us. She had always just let him barrel right over us after all.

"I, ummm, you're glad?"

"Of course I am, honey. I know I never stood up for you and your brothers against your father. I just need you to understand that I wasn't in a place where I could. That's all over now, he's gone and I don't have to watch what I say to the five of you."

She tossed her gaze over her shoulder to where Brandon and Tristan were dealing with my father's body, several Clipper males helping them. I followed her line of sight and shuddered slightly, still not really comfortable with the amount of killing I had done in the last year. Sure it was only twice, but that was two deaths too many as far as I was concerned. Whether they deserved it or not, I hated that the two men had died at my jaws, that their blood was on me. I let out a heavy sigh as I watched my two middle brothers and their friends bury my father. My mother moved to stand on my left, Frost in her place at my right as Tristan headed our way.

"Hey Kyn."

"Hey Tris. All taken care of?"

He gave me a short nod and then ran his hand through his light brown hair, allowing me a moment to wonder how the five of us all looked so different. It was a strange and disconnected thought pattern, but it was how my mind was coping with what had happened. I was strawberry blond, darkening a bit over the last several months into a redder hue with pale blue eyes. My father had been, I had to take that in for a moment, had been, he was gone now, he had been dirty blond with steel gray eyes. My mother had deep brown hair the color of chocolate, but held the same pale blue eyes I had myself. Dante had a sweep of dark, almost black hair and the same pale, ice blue eyes my mother and I shared.

Brandon looked just like Dane, dirty blonde hair, silvery steel colored eyes, but was built a bit more solidly, sporting more muscle than Dane ever had. Tristan was stark blond, more like Abbey and also had our fathers' steel eyes that always seemed to hold just a little mischief in their depths. Shane was the youngest and looked nothing like any of the rest of us with his shaggy mop of sharp red hair and bright emerald green eyes.

I actually managed to smile as the brother that I had been thinking about approached us and I once again wondered if we were all actually related. Dante, Brandon and Tristan had spent several years when we were younger teasing Shane and I, telling us that we weren't really their siblings, that mom and dad had found us in the woods. I had wondered back then if maybe they were right and it was a sentiment that I wished were true again right now. It would make what I had done easier to deal with, easier to process than it was currently which would help my sanity out a bit. I sighed and turned my attention back to Tristan, realizing that he had been talking and I had completely missed whatever he had said.

"I'm sorry, Tris, I was in my head. What did you say?"

"It's okay, I was asking what you wanted us to do now."

"Huh? What do you mean?"

I had the feeling that I was in a bit of shock since I couldn't manage to understand what it was he was trying to ask me.

"Our Alpha is dead, Kyndle. That leaves you in charge. What do you want us to do?"

My heart raced, my breath shuddering out as I finally grasped the reality of what I had done and where it left the two packs. The Clippers and the Riders were both large packs, honestly too large to try and combine them into a single pack. Thanks to what had just happened however, there might not be another choice and combining the packs might have to happen. I glanced around me, taking in the members of both packs that had attended the challenge. Most of the Clipper members in attendance looked as in shock as I had just been and I had the feeling that once that wore off, they wouldn't be very happy.

I was expecting a healthy dose of anger with a side of attitude and just a dash of defiance tossed in for good measure. I let my eyes wander back to my brother and finally considered what my next step should be, mulling it over for a minute. I had been around and around in my head, and even with a lot of Frost's help over the last several months as we waited for my father to follow through with the challenge, we had never landed on a solid solution we thought would actually work.

"I honestly don't know, Tristan. I'll just have to wing it and hope that we can all get it right. Where do you and Brandon stand?"

I hated having to ask, but I needed to know if I would have to deal with two of my brothers being against me on this. He let out a chuckle and shook his head, threw a look over his shoulder at Brandon and then shrugged as he turned back to me.

"I can't speak for him, but I'm with you on this sis. Whatever you need, I'll do what I can to support it." I must have looked stunned at the comment because he laughed, actually laughed at me and then reached over and gave my left shoulder a shove. "You should see your face! Is it that shocking that I would back my little sister?"

"Honestly? Yeah, it is a little shocking to hear. I mean, you stayed, both of you."

"Of course we stayed, Kyn. He was unstable and ridiculous, but he was still our father. Besides, we couldn't leave mom alone to deal with his anger. It went a bit through the roof when you left and only got worse after Shane followed you. When Dante defected, he lost it a little bit, and if Brandon and I hadn't stayed to give him a vent for it all, he would have taken it out on her."

I watched him reach over and put a hand on our mother's shoulder and just nodded as a reply. What could I possibly say in response to that since I couldn't very well argue that it was a lie. Dane had been an angry bastard on his best days, when he was truly pissed off, we did everything we could to stay out of sight and avoid him at all costs.

"Okay, I can understand that, but... Please don't take this wrong, either of you, I won't apologize for leaving, or for rejecting Cameron. No matter how bad he may have gotten afterward."

I looked between my two family members as Brandon joined us, the look on his face telling me that he had overheard most of what we had been saying.

"We don't expect you to apologize for that, Kyndle. You did what you had to do." Brandon had spoken, but Tristan and my mother both nodded in agreement and I let it sink in. "Look, I can't imagine what it must have felt like to have someone take your choice, your future away from you like he did. Knowing that you had found your mate and couldn't even tell your family, then to find out that your own father was basically selling you off to pay an old debt, I can't even begin to know how that felt for you. While I can see where he was coming from, I didn't agree with his choice and I lost what little respect was left there. I can't believe that he would have done that to one of us." He indicated himself and my three other brothers with a wave of his hand. "The fact that he would do it to you was shocking."

"Of course he wouldn't have done it to any of you, you're all male and so you were all allowed your own choices in life. What you wanted mattered to him in at least some way, I was never that lucky." There was no anger behind the words any longer, that had faded months ago when I had finally bonded to Frost. He had attempted to cut the happiness out of my life and I had fought back, had won and that was what mattered. Brandon nodded a little as my mother gave my shoulder a squeeze, a gesture I hadn't been expecting. "I want to be different. I won't be like him, I don't expect anyone to follow me because they're afraid of me."

"We know you don't and that's something to be respected. Should we look at combining the packs in the next few weeks? Which territory should we use? What happens to the pack structures now?" I sighed, my hands moving up so I could rub my temples with my fingertips, attempting to hold an impending headache at bay. "I know this is a lot to deal with all in a small space of time, Kyndle, but we'll help as much as we can." I dropped my hands so I could look at him and saw the truth in Brandon's silvery gaze, instantly feeling lighter than I had a few moments earlier.

"I know you will, we just need to take this a step at a time. First, we need to get the packs together; Clipper land has the largest clearing, get everyone there in two hours. We need to make sure everyone is aware of what happened and what it means."

"And then?"

I looked at Dante as he stepped up between Brandon and Tristan and shook my head.

"And then we give the packs a choice, stay and follow me as their Alpha."

"Or?"

My mother posed the word as a question, but something about the way she said it made me think that she knew what the answer would be.

"Or they can leave. I won't force anyone that doesn't want an eighteen year old female Alpha to follow me, but I won't allow them to stay and cause problems either. They submit to my leadership or they remove themselves from pack territory, my territory. That goes for both packs and the land belonging to each. I have the feeling we may lose several members of both packs and that may actually get us to a manageable number we can combine. I guess we'll just have to wait and see."

CHAPTER NINE

I HAD to admit that I was a little shocked when I stepped into the clearing on Clipper land two hours later to find almost the entirety of both packs present. I had expected a show of mass disrespect from the Clippers at the very least. Knowing they had at least bothered to heed my call to gather helped my confidence a bit. I stepped from the tree line, Frost at my side, Abbey, Kyle, Austin and Rebecca just behind us, my brothers and mother following a few feet behind. My siblings and mother stopped just a few feet into the clearing, allowing the rest of us to continue toward the middle. It was time to confront the packs and find out how many I would be left with once it was over.

I stopped near the middle of the space and took a few moments to look over the gathered crowd. At first glance it had appeared that everyone was present and upon closer inspection, that still seemed to ring true. I felt Frost's hand in mine and smiled, knowing that I could do what needed to be done to start getting everything sorted out.

"Thank you all for coming, I really appreciate you all showing up despite the events that took place earlier this evening." A few grumbles and faint chatter swept through the crowd, but quieted quickly, allowing me to continue. "The next few weeks won't be easy, but I believe that if we work together, we can all make it through the trying times facing us. While I hope that we can all learn to accept this new dynamic that we find ourselves facing, I know that there will be some of you that don't agree with the change in leadership and I'm offering a chance to deal with that without conflict.

"This first month will be a time of transition, a time when those of you who don't like this new setup can remove yourselves from it. Anyone who wishes to leave will be allowed to do so without any arguments or questions from myself or Frost. You will be released and allowed to go on your way, we may even be able to help you contact members of other packs you might know and work out relocating you. For those who choose to stay, please understand what that will mean, for both you and the new pack dynamic. We will all have to learn how to live together, how to interact and work side by side. I will do everything that I can to mediate any disputes that come from the blending we're going to have to go through.

"You are all welcome and actually encouraged to stay in your homes and keep your current jobs, Frost and I will do what we can to visit each of you over the coming weeks. During these visits we will address any concerns you may have and hopefully ease any fears that may surface. I won't begin to suggest that this will be easy, these two packs, while close in proximity, have always been vastly different and we know that there are bound to be conflicts. All we ask is that you please bring any disputes to us rather than attempting to deal with them on your own. I would also like to announce that this newly joined pack will have Co-Betas in Abbey and Austin. You should all know them both well. Feel free to bring your issues to them as well if Frost and I aren't available. Thank you all for your time, Frost and I as well as our Betas will hang behind for a while to answer questions."

We stood and watched as most of the crowd started to disperse and wondered how many questions we would end up answering. There was a decent chance that we would be standing in the clearing calming the fears and worries of the packs for the next few hours. I was already exhausted and the mostly healed injuries Dane had given me during the fight were itchy and begging to have the fabric off of them. We took a couple of camp chairs that Abbey and Kyle brought to us, thankful that my best friend had managed to think ahead and pack them. At least we would all have somewhere to sit as we dealt with what was bound to be a lot of panic and worry.

The crowd of former Clippers wanting to speak to their new leaders was growing by the second as the Rider members headed for home. They still weren't behind us one hundred percent, but they were over the shock at least, this was all new for my old pack. I knew that most of what we would deal with over the next few days, maybe even weeks would be pack members who had known me my entire life trying to grasp me leading them. The last most of them remembered of me was a slightly wild, somewhat unruly teenager who liked getting into mischief. They would have to get used to this new side of me. The undisciplined girl I had been was gone and had been replaced by a young woman ready to lead, that would take some time to show itself true to them.

As predicted, it was hours later by the time everyone had cleared out and headed home and I felt ragged. I was exhausted and ready to go home, crawl into bed and do my best to stay there for a day or two, not that I had any chance of that scenario being likely. I had two packs to try and manage and no way to know how long it would take things to sort themselves out. Not to mention having no idea how many members of my old pack, now my new pack, would decide to leave. I hated to admit it, but the more of them that left, the easier it would be on Frost and I to manage the blending of the two packs.

I let out a sigh as I leaned my head back and closed my eyes, rubbing my face with both hands. Movement caught my attention, but the scent accompanying it made a small, tired grin tug at the corners of my lips as I heard Frost kneel in front of me. Her hands rested on my knees and I sat up so I could look at her, a gentle smile on her face. I reached out and pressed my hand to her cheek, my thumb moving to trace over her lower lip. We sat there for a few moments, letting the comfortable, easy silence stretch out between us. She leaned in after a minute and kissed me, her hands sliding up to my hips as mine eased into her hair. We didn't linger long, both too tired and far too exposed out in the clearing on Clipper land to take it any further.

Once we pulled apart, I moved to stand up and offered her my hand, which she took as she got to her feet. The clearing was totally empty except the two of us, our betas and their mates having left a few minutes earlier to give us some time alone. We made our way back toward Rider land and our home, but as we stepped over the boundary between the two territories I paused. Frost gave my hand a squeeze and I glanced over at her, thinking for a moment before I took a slow breath.

"I know you're tired, I am too, but there's something I think I need to do. You don't have to come with me if you'd rather go get some sleep."

"Wherever you're going, I'm going too, Kyndle. Lead the way."

I smiled at her, constantly finding new ways every single day that I was glad to have her in my life. She always had my back and supported me even when she didn't know what I was dragging her into. I nodded and then turned and led us back to the clearing where the challenge had taken place earlier that evening. I stopped as we stepped from the trees and just stared at the space for a minute, the ground still torn up from the fight. There wasn't any visual evidence of what had happened, but the scent of blood and death was still strong in space and it made my heart ache a little.

I set my jaw, squared my shoulders and started toward the spot where my brothers had buried Dane, dropping Frost's hand when I was just a few feet away. I walked right up to the spot, covered up well since a pronounced grave-like mound might draw attention to any humans wandering through the space. It might not be visible to the average person, but I knew it was there, knew what was just a few feet below the dirt. I eased down to one knee and reached down, putting one hand to the ground as I forced myself to remember what I'd done. I had pushed it all aside to deal with pack business for the evening, but I still had a lot to process.

I didn't even realize I had started crying until a few tears dripped off my nose and landed in the dirt, darkening it slightly. Once I knew it was happening, there was no stopping it and I just closed my eyes and let them fall as I shook my head.

"You stubborn bastard..." The words were strained, a rough whisper that could have been swept away by the smallest breeze. Frost dropped to her knees beside me as I said them and pressed a hand to my back, but kept quiet, silent support as I dealt with my emotions. "Why couldn't you just back down from something for once in your life? I hated you, my entire life I just wanted to get the hell away from you. But I never wanted you dead... Why did you make me do this?"

I went silent after that, not having anything else to say and just let the tears fall until they ran dry. I sucked in a deep breath as Frost shifted and pulled me into a hug, my head against her shoulder as I let the last edges of it all clear. Once I felt stable again, I gave her shoulder a tap and she pulled back, stood and helped me to my feet. She ran her fingers through my hair, still not saying a word, allowing me to decide when I was ready to talk. I appreciated the silence and after a few moments I managed a smile as I reached up and chucked her lightly under her chin with my index finger.

"Thank you."

"For what babe?"

She looked legitimately confused by the thanks and I couldn't help but shake my head as I smiled at her.

"Being you. Being here to support me while I deal with this."

"Of course. Are you okay?"

She stared at me, genuine concern on her face and I considered the question for a moment.

"I'm honestly not sure. I think I'm still processing it all. I'm better than I was earlier at the very least."

"Well, that's something."

I nodded with a small, sad-sounding chuckle and then sighed heavily and glanced over my shoulder one last time before looking back to her.

"Yeah. Come on, let's go home. I'm exhausted."

"I'll bet."

With that we turned and left the clearing, headed for the place we had made our home in silence. I would have a lot to deal with over the next few weeks. No, that thinking was wrong, I wouldn't have things to deal with, we would. Frost and I would handle it all together, just like we did everything. I had to keep reminding myself that she was right there by my side through it all, I didn't have to go through it alone and I could lean on her. A real, happy smile crossed my face at the thought as we stepped through our front door and made our way upstairs to get some much needed and well-earned rest.

CHAPTER TEN

SIX DAYS had passed since the night of the challenge and damn close to half the Clippers had already begun talking about leaving the pack and relocating. I had told them all that I would allow the choice and I wasn't about to go back on that, but it didn't make me like it. Several Rider members had decided to defect as well and while I hated the idea of the packs falling apart, I knew that it would be best to slim out our numbers a little if I was expecting to do my job as Alpha properly. I was taking some much needed down time, something that we had all had very little of since the week before.

I was leaned back against the couch on our living room floor, Frost sitting between my legs, cuddled up against me as a fire crackled in the fireplace in front of us. I was holding her close with my arms around her waist and my chin on her shoulder, but my mind was off in another place. She seemed to realize that I was lost in thought and just sat there, relaxed against me, not speaking and allowing me the chance to work through what was on my mind. I had spent a lot of time in my head the last several months, going over everything that had led us to this point we were at again and again. So much had happened that had everything to do with the choices I had made. Choices which had far-reaching consequences and had changed the lives of over a hundred individuals.

I still wasn't sure how I felt about that fact, but I had to accept that I couldn't change it now, I probably wouldn't have changed it even when I could have. Even had I known almost three years ago where my choice to pursue Frost would land us, I wouldn't have chosen any differently. I was confident in that fact because I had known, even back then, that I had met the one I was meant to be with forever. As much turmoil and chaos as our relationship had managed to cause, I still wouldn't give her up for anything. A small smile eased across my face as I once again realized that I would never have to give her up, that we were bonded and no one could change that.

A loud knock on the front door ripped me from my thoughts and wiped the smile off my face, replacing it with a look of confusion. A few pack members had come by the house over the last few days, but most of them called first and the rest tended to use the doorbell. I turned my eyes down to Frost and she looked as confused as I was, but she shifted around to stand and made her way to the door. I heard her open it then the sounds of voices reached me and I pulled up to my feet to see who was interrupting our evening.

"Kyndle, honey, would you come in here please."

My brows furrowed down at the tone in my mate's voice, unsure and just a little worried and I quickly moved to join her in the entryway. I froze as I reached the doorway, seeing why she sounded so worried and I felt my stomach do a little flip flop.

"Kyndle, it's been years." The deep baritone that met my ears came from a man that I had known my entire life, but never really liked. Maxwell was a massive man, well over six and half feet, I had to guess somewhere around six foot nine inches or so. His dark skin was evenly toned and wrapped over well-defined muscles that had seemed to multiply since I had seen him last around three years earlier. He was bald now, probably by choice since he hadn't been showing any signs of hair loss at our last encounter. His well-tended goatee was still jet black, showing none of the sixty-seven years he had under his belt.

Part of the charm of being a werewolf was slowed aging, though some of our kind managed to worry themselves into aged looks just like humans. With healthy, active lifestyles, we could look twenty-five well into our eighties. His sharp, pale gray eyes were still as shocking against his dark skin even after all these years and still held an unsettling look in them, like he could see right through me.

"Maxwell." Frost looked between the two of us, the worry no longer showing on her face, but I knew she was still feeling it. "To what do we owe this visit? Are you alone or is the rest of the Elder Council with you?"

Maxwell was a member of a group who kept the packs in the northwest in line and made what they considered important decisions for the packs. It was the council that was pushing for our kind to be out and public knowledge in the United States and they had proven again and again over the decades that they had their own interests at heart, not those of the packs. If he was here alone then he might have just heard what happened and come to see what was going on. He and Dane had been friends for years. If the entire council was on hand we could be in for trouble and that was something I just didn't have the energy for.

"Is a visit from us really that bad, child?" I cringed inwardly at the voice that hit me like a slap in the face, making sure I didn't show how uncomfortable this situation was becoming. I turned to face the owner of the voice, a small but solid man my height with shockingly red hair streaked white here and there and deep, clear green eyes. His presence could only mean that the rest of the council wasn't far behind and this wasn't a social visit.

"It depends on what the reasoning behind the visit is, Seamus. If you're here it can't be anything I'll enjoy which removes it from the realm of pleasant rather effectively." He raised one bushy red eyebrow at me as Maxwell chuckled, the deep sound reverberating off the walls.

"Well, I don't know how I feel about that assessment, but if that's how you feel."

It was how I felt, I had never known Seamus to make random social calls like the rest of the council often did. Even when the others made social visits, they generally did so alone, not as a group so this couldn't be anything that would end well, I was sure.

"Well, come on in."

I waved them into the house, pointing them toward the living room as the other members of the council appeared on the porch. I welcomed each of them despite not being the least bit happy to see them and got them all settled in our living room. Maxwell was seated in my oversized recliner, the only chair in the room that would actually accommodate his size, while Seamus had settled in Frost's armchair. Damon, the youngest of the group at only fifty-two, had settled his six foot two inch frame on our loveseat, taking it over as his dark brown eyes scanned the room, his long chocolate hair pulled back from his face in a loose ponytail. Xander flopped his six foot tall body down onto one end of the sofa, his hazel eyes flicking from item to item as he took in the room, his shaggy dark blond hair falling in his eyes.

The last of the group into the room was Dax, the oldest by far at almost a hundred and two and the leader of the northwest council of elders. He was an intimidating man though not really in size since he was only a rather average five foot eleven. His presence, however, was massive and seemed to fill the entire room around us. He didn't bother to sit, choosing instead to stand in the middle of the living room like he owned the place. That pissed me off a little, watching him stand there like my space, my home with Frost, was his. I tamped the feeling down, knowing that snapping at him would get me nowhere and turned my attention back to Seamus.

Dax might be the leader of the council, but Seamus was his right hand, his voice and he would be the one speaking. Our leader rarely spoke and it was said that when he did, it was never with good news and often left those present broken and terrified. I wasn't sure if I believed all of that, but I didn't have anything to go on so I couldn't really argue the validity of the stories.

"Okay, girlie." Seamus paused when I shot him a look for the term he had decided to use with me and he just chuckled. "Down girl, I wasn't taking a shot, ease off. Let's start again, shall we? Kyndle, we obviously heard about what happened here last week. We spent the last few days trying to come to a decision on how to best handle the situation at hand."

"Meaning what? There's nothing to handle, it's already handled, trust me."

"No, I don't think it is. You may think it is, but the fact is that what you are trying to do here just won't work." His look had taken on a hard edge as he spoke, that intensity made him intimidating despite his size. I didn't speak again, simply quirked a brow at him and waited for him to continue, knowing that this wasn't going anywhere that I was going to like. "Despite what the northeast and southwest councils allow in their packs, we aren't ready to allow leadership like yours in ours." Leadership like ours, the hostility I felt in those words may have been imagined, but I doubted it.

"Like ours? And what kind of leadership is that exactly? Young? Female?"

"Yes, and yes but also... Well, there's no other way to put this than to just say it. The whole..."

"The whole Lesbian thing." I cut him off before he could

finish the sentence, really not wanting to hear it coming out of his mouth. He nodded and I felt myself start to fume, I was losing my temper and I needed to keep it under control unless I wanted some serious trouble. "I see. So due to the fact that Frost and I happen to be young, female and together rather than having male mates means we aren't fit to lead in your eyes? Is that what you're saying?"

"That's pretty much exactly what we're saying. You girls are so young, Frost won't be nineteen for another two weeks and you have about three months until that point yourself, Kyndle." I just gave him an exasperated sigh, I knew my own damn birthday as well as Frost's.

"So what are you getting at exactly?"

"You will remain in the territory until suitable replacements can be found to lead both packs, and then the two of you will leave." My jaw dropped and a small gasp from my right let me know that Frost had just had the same reaction.

"Are you serious? You're taking the packs that I won the right to lead, by your own laws I might add, away from me?"

"They should have never been yours to begin with. The right of challenge was never meant to be taken up by females." I scoffed at the words as he said them, finding the very thought of what they were suggesting ridiculous, not to mention sexist.

"This is ridiculous. You can't do this. It's my right to lead these packs and I won't just walk away."

"You will, or you will pay for your disrespect of this council with your life." The deep and unfamiliar voice drew my eyes to Dax, shock reaching my features as I realized that he had not only spoken, but that he had threatened to kill me if I fought them on the matter.

"You would kill me, a strong Alpha that has already proven myself in challenge twice over, just so you can have males leading these packs?" The slow, determined nod that he gave me chilled me right to the bone and I knew that he wouldn't hesitate to end my life right where I stood. "Damn. Can I say or do anything to change your minds?"

"No, the choice is made and it was unanimous. We all agreed that you and Frost shouldn't be allowed to keep your leadership of the Clipper and Rider packs. We'll gather the remaining male candidates for Alpha of both packs and decide on one for each over the next few weeks. We suggest that you work on packing your things and finding somewhere else to go. As soon as both packs are settled with new Alphas, the two of you will cease to be welcome here."

"Here as in the territories of the packs or here as in *your* territories?" Frost had voiced the question before I could manage and I gave her a sad smile before I turned back to Seamus.

"The northwest territories are no longer your home girls. Find somewhere else. As for your friends in California, don't bother asking them, they are being dealt with for harboring you when you ran away last year." I was all at once worried about where we would go and terrified at the prospect of Barkley and Hank being reprimanded for helping us. This night just kept getting worse and I wanted them all out of my house so I could pretend none of this had happened. "We'll make our rounds and gather the candidates over the next several days so we can get to know them. We suggest that you refrain from making any decisions that concern the packs and urge you to stay out of contact with the Alpha line males in both packs until our choices are made."

I was getting more irate with every second he continued speaking, but there was nothing that I could do to change what was happening.

"Fine. Whatever you want, not like I have a choice." I hated not having a choice in the path my life was taking, it was half of why I had fought Dane so hard. This time there would be no fight, no arguments, the very real threat of being removed from the ranks of the living had taken the wind out of my sails for the moment. When it came to the council, if I disobeyed, there would be no challenges, no fair match up with a fight. I would be executed and that would be the end of it as far as everyone was concerned. For my sake, Frost's sake, I had to do as they told me. I stayed put in the spot I'd claimed in the living room as the five council members showed themselves out and Frost locked the door. I had to accept their choice, but I definitely didn't have to like it. I was fuming. I had no idea where we were supposed to go or even how we were supposed to get there, not to mention having no idea who would leave with us.

I felt a small nudge on my arm and lifted it so Frost could slip under it and cuddle into my side, bringing a little smile to my face despite the anger. I wrapped my arm around her and pulled her over in front of me, hugging her tight as I nuzzled my face in against her neck. "Where the hell are we supposed to go, Frost?"

"I don't know, but we'll figure it out. Maybe we can head north." It was an idea, and a decent one at that since none of the councils in the United States could dictate anything that happened across the northern border. I wondered if there were councils set up in Canada as well that might hinder us in finding a place there to settle. I didn't voice the questions, just let them settle into my mind for later retrieval, right now I just needed this, Frost in my arms and silence. She seemed to sense that and rather than trying to continue talking to me she simply adjusted away from me enough to get me to settle back in where I had been before the knock on our door. I leaned back against the couch and waited until she was back where she had been a few minutes before, then wrapped my arms around her. My eyes had just closed when I heard the front door and wondered what could possibly be going on now.

"Hey guys, sorry to just burst in on you, but I saw the council and knew something was up, what did they say?" I was too drained to go over it all again so I just gave Frost a squeeze and she proceeded to spend the next few minutes filling Abbey in. Once she finally finished telling her what had happened, I decided to join the conversation and we spent several minutes going over what we could do, what the next step should be. We decided on the best course of action and then sent Abbey to fill Kyle, Austin and Rebecca in on the plans. She would get things in order to get passports for herself and Kyle so that they could drive the two trucks that the small group owned across the border.

Our belongings would be packed into the trucks with the two cars being towed behind them for the trip. The rest of us would be making the journey in wolf form and working out the details when we reached the other side. There were plenty of holes in the plan that could cause problems, but we didn't have much choice and had very little time. Our documents would be faked since our kind were rarely born in hospitals and only bothered with human documentation when it was required. Even then it was normally less than real. It would be hard to explain someone who looked thirty walking around with a birth certificate issued eighty years ago.

If they could manage, they would obtain them for all of us, but two were easier to manage than a dozen or so, we would take what we could get. I just had to hope that my mother and brothers would be coming with us when we left. Abbey would be talking to them for me as well since I had been all but ordered to refrain from contact with at least three of my four brothers. I heaved a sigh and relaxed back against the couch since there was nothing left to do but try and not worry. Frost left me to toss a couple more logs on our fire and stoke it, making sure it was going strong. She sat there for a moment, deep in thought and then replaced the poker, pushed herself up and headed for the kitchen.

I settled back and closed my eyes, not worrying about where she had gone, she never went far and I knew she would be back shortly. I heard her come back a couple minutes later and opened one eye to see what she had been doing. She had the electric kettle in one hand, two mugs dangling from the handles in the other and a box of instant hot chocolate mix under her arm. I grinned at her and adjusted enough so I could hold onto a mug without spilling steaming water all over myself, or my mate for that matter. She handed me one of the mugs, dumped a packet of the mix into it and then plugged in the kettle and turned it on.

She wandered back into the kitchen as the water heated, returning a few moments later with a bag of miniature marshmallows and a gallon of water. She knew exactly how to help ease my worries and I was thankful for that more and more every day. I waited for her to settle in and pull one of the throw blankets over us then leaned in and pecked her on the cheek, earning me a little smile.

"Thank you."

"You're welcome."

She didn't bother asking me what I was thanking her for, she knew without needing me to say it out loud.

"I love you."

"I love you too, Kyndle."

She leaned over and pressed her lips to mine for a few seconds until the kettle started to squeal at us. She added the water to both our mugs and then turned and leaned back into my embrace, eyes trained on the fire. We sipped hot chocolate in silence for the next hour, just enjoying each other's company, not feeling the need to fill the silence with idle chatter. Eventually the water ran out, the drink mix was gone and the fire had died down so we relocated to the bedroom. The day had been a trying one, just like the last few weeks and months we had just survived and we were both exhausted. It didn't take long after we had settled into our bed for me to drift off, hoping as the darkness took over that my sleep would be dream free.

CHAPTER ELEVEN

I WOKE with a start to the sound of someone pounding on the front door and grumbled a little at the intrusion into my morning. I rolled over and reached out, huffing as I found Frost's side of the bed not only empty, but cold as well. Apparently, she had been up for a while and I had been so deep in slumber that I hadn't even noticed when she'd left our bed. At least that meant that she was up and could answer the door, which meant that I could turn over and go back to sleep. I was in the process of doing just that when the bedroom door opened and my mate's scent wafted over me, leaving a small smile on my face.

I heard her pad lightly over to the bed, but pulled the blankets over my head, not wanting to deal with whatever it was that had someone knocking on the door so early in the morning. "Come on honey, you need to get up." I growled a little and shook my head under the layers of fabric, I was still tired and not in the mood to deal with anyone. "Kyndle, seriously, you aren't five, get up. The council is here."

That definitely set me in a mood where I didn't want to get up and deal with it, not if those bastards were involved. Sadly, I didn't have much choice, keeping them waiting too long was almost as bad as defying them in their eyes. I let out a huff, threw the blankets back and turned to look up at my mate, the expression on my face not a happy one.

"I know, I know, but there's nothing you can do about it, they want to talk to you, now."

It had been ten days since the council had shown up on our doorstep and told me that I was having the packs I had fought to lead taken away from me. I had been dreading this day since they had walked out of the house and I knew that their presence couldn't be anything I'd want to hear. I dragged myself out of bed and yanked open the nearest suitcase, looking around the room as I changed. Everything we owned was in bags or boxes, the whole house completely devoid of anything personal.

We'd spent the last week and a half preparing to leave, knowing that it could happen any time, without warning. That time had apparently come and I couldn't help feeling like my entire life was being swept out from under me. I yanked on my shoes, finger-combed my hair and met Frost by the bedroom door where she had been standing, looking over the room.

"I'm really going to miss this place."

The pain in her voice was evident and I felt like my heart was breaking as I watched her look over the room that we had shared for the last several months. The house had been the first place that we had called home as a bonded pair, but it was obviously not meant to be our final destination.

"I know baby, I'll miss it too. This house actually felt like home." She nodded in agreement and then sighed as I took her hand, giving it a light squeeze that brought her attention to me. "Let's go get this over with, find out who they're replacing me with." I watched her brows furrow down at the comment and I knew she was just as upset by the council's decision as I was. It wasn't right and it definitely wasn't fair, but in our world, their word was law and trying to fight it never ended well. Besides, hadn't people always told us growing up that life wasn't fair anyway?

"I finished packing this morning, at least everything we were planning on taking with us. I know there are things we'll have to replace later, but we can worry about that when the time comes."

I nodded and took a deep breath, holding it for a few seconds before I turned, exhaled sharply and led her toward the door. We made our way down into the living room, now cluttered with boxes and bags that were packed and ready to be loaded up. I took a moment to glance around at the boxed clutter that had been our home and felt my stomach knot up. I didn't have time to deal with the hurt with so many other things going on so I tamped it down and turned my attention to Seamus.

"Okay, Seamus, let's have it."

"Have what?" I really wasn't in the mood to deal with his annoying personality quirks so early in the day, or at all these days really. He needed to just get over himself and get to the point already, tell me why he was standing in my living room. Not that I could tell him to stop with the bullshit and just get on with it, he'd just get worse if I took that approach. Instead I just gave him a look, one eyebrow raised and asking him to get on with it already, put me out of my misery. I felt Frost step up beside me and a quick glance her direction from the corner of my eye showed her in a tight stance, arms crossed over her chest and a look on her face that mirrored my own.

She was just as fed up with their crap as I was and if people thought I was bad when I lost my temper, they should really meet the end of Frost's fuse. With me, I was almost always ticked off about something and my temper was quick and burned out fast. Frost, on the other hand was slow to lose her temper, but when she did it burned for a while and she wouldn't rest until she had righted whatever she saw as wrong. "Alright, alright." He had seen the expression on my mate's face and had apparently decided to not push it any further than he already had.

"You win, we've made our decision. We had originally wanted to replace you in both packs with your brothers, Dante and Brandon." My breath caught in my chest, my heart dropped and my stomach tightened at the words. I shouldn't have been shocked that he would want my family to maintain leadership of the Clippers, or to take over the Riders, I just hadn't been prepared to actually hear it. "Sadly, they both turned us down, as did your brother Tristan." I probably shouldn't have felt as relieved as I was at the news. I knew if anyone could keep these packs together, it would be my brothers. I couldn't help the relief and love that washed over me hearing that my brothers had my back in all this though. "Instead we decided to go a rather odd route. Daniel has been given the Clipper pack and Gregory has been hunted down and handed control of the Rider pack." I felt my blood boil a little, felt the heat and tension coming off of Frost beside me and let my muscles tense up.

"I can't believe you would put those two in charge of anything. I can accept that you think I can't handle this, it's just part of your narrow-minded beliefs, but those two, Gregory most of all, are toxic. They won't do anything but dig these two packs into the ground. I wouldn't think that you would jeopardize your two strongest packs that way, guess I would be wrong." I was so far beyond pissed off that I could hardly see straight, and I wasn't about to keep it all bottled up, just most of it.

"Well, the packs are no longer your problem." Maxwell's voice cut through the room and left me fuming even further, these two packs would never be my problem, but I would *always* see them as my responsibility. I stamped down on the anger trying to rise inside me, attempting to quiet the wolf as she growled and paced just below the surface.

"You're right, no longer my problem. We'll be out of here as soon as we can get the trucks over and load them up."

The members of the council nodded their understanding and then vacated the house, much like we would be doing soon. I called Abbey to let her know that we were ready to go and then Frost and I started moving everything down onto the front porch for easier loading. It was over a week into January and I could hardly believe that Christmas and New Years had passed us by so quickly. I had barely had the time to register the holidays this year, there had been so much going on around us. I hoped that next year would be different, sighing as I set the last box from the kitchen on the front steps. I straightened up, stretching out my back to pop it as Abbey pulled up, Kyle a few seconds behind her. I managed a small smile and a wave at her, but then a look of confusion took over my features as a few other vehicles pulled up behind them.

"Hey lady, ready to start loading up and get out of here?" I just stood there, dumbfounded and unable to speak as several more cars and trucks parked along the road leading to the house. "Hello, Earth to Kyndle, you in there?"

"Oh, yeah, sorry Abs. What is this?" She gave me a sheepish grin, tossed a look over her shoulder as Dante emerged from one of the trucks and joined us on the porch.

"Hey sis!"

"Hey, what's going on?"

"Well, a bunch of us heard what happened and decided that we're not okay with the council's decision so, we're leaving with you." I was stunned to the point that I couldn't speak, something that didn't happen often and that made Dante chuckle at me. I looked between the vehicles parked along the road for a few moments before I returned my attention to my brother. I felt Frost step up beside me, leaned into her a little as her arm slid around my ecame more pronounced. After a couple minutes, he looked away with a soft growl and I couldn't help the smirk that tweaked my lips at the corners.

"Enough of this." I hadn't expected Dax to speak and his voice made my eye twitch a little bit before I turned my attention to him. "You have been removed by this council and you *will* leave. Now."

"Who gave this council ultimate authority? I don't remember anyone in my generation voting on your leadership."

"Voting on leadership is something that Humans do, child. Our kind, we are different, our world is different and you know as much. Why do you insist on defying us?"

"Because you're wrong. I'm capable of leading these packs, at least one of them. Leave me the Rider pack, I won the right to lead here and the pack has no other viable Alpha."

I knew Greg was sitting behind me fuming, ticked that I had just stated that he wasn't worthy of leading the pack he was being handed.

"And the Clippers?"

At least he had asked me, I had honestly just expected his eye to twitch and his face to turn red as he told me to get the hell out.

"If I stay, Dante will as well. I'm sure that he would be more than happy to whip that pack into shape."

"He already turned us down."

"He turned you down because you're forcing me out. If I stay and it's me that asks him to take over, he will."

Dax actually seemed to think that through for a moment and I could see the panic in Greg's eyes as he started to worry that I might have gotten through to the old man.

"No. No we can't allow that to happen. You can't stay, can't lead the pack."

"Why? I know the reasons that you've told me, but none of them make much sense. None of them render me incapable of actually leading. It's all just your opinions on the matter. You say because I'm young, Cameron was only nineteen when he took over the Rider pack. You say because I'm female, packs all through New England and the southern states have female Alphas and they're doing just fine. As for the fact that Frost and I are bonded, I don't see how having a strong, well matched, bonded Alpha pair that have the best interests of the pack at heart is a bad thing. Explain to me how that's bad for the pack, please?"

"The packs in our territories are old fashioned, Kyndle. They

waist and waited for someone else to speak. "Look, Kyn, I kr
met with a lot of resistance when you took over the Riders :
same would have been true with our old pack to some degi
not everyone was against you. There are a lot of us willing to
with you if you leave, I think you should make one last effoi
and keep your place here. We're behind you, we'll stand w
whether you stay or go, know that."

I had to admit that it was probably worth one last ditcl
to try and maintain my place, my leadership.

"I guess I shouldn't just walk away without a fight, huh?"

I felt Frost's arm tighten around me and watched a
smile take over my brother's face.

"Now that's my little sister! Go on, Abbey and Austin w
you to them, the rest of us will load up, just in case."

I let out a soft chuckle as I punched him lightly
shoulder then started down the steps, Frost's arm still arou
waist. We piled into our car and headed off to find the coi
had the feeling that I was just going to get myself into more t
but Dante was right, I had to at least try. It turned out tl
council members were meeting with Daniel and Greg at the
pack meeting hall. The looks on their faces when we steppe
the space were a mixture of shock, confusion and irritation.
that they weren't used to being disobeyed, even to this small
and they weren't happy about it in the least. Greg looked
pissed than anyone else in the room and I could understand
had kicked him out and he never wanted to see me agai
feeling was mutual.

"What are you doing here?"

The venom dripping from Greg's tone was so thick you
almost cut through it. I turned my gaze on him, my expression
collected and as neutral as I could manage given the circumsta:

"I'm taking one last chance to stake my claim on the pacl
very packs that are being taken from me without legitimate
rather unfairly, not to mention against my wishes as rightful /
I can't just walk away and let this happen without at least try
change your minds. These packs are mine by right, I fougl
them, I bled for them... I killed for them."

Greg glared at me, hoping to stare me down, sure that I v
be intimidated and look away from him. I wasn't scared of hii
didn't intimidate me and I wouldn't be the one looking av
stared him down, my expression still fairly neutral as his

aren't ready for your kind of partnership, this kind of bond. If we allow this, the other Alphas will hear about it, they will rebel and make our jobs that much more difficult."

So that was it, the whole big sticky deal that was making them run me off, that was taking my packs from me.

"So it has less to do with me and more about saving your own asses, about making sure your lives are easier. That it?" He didn't say anything, but the expressions the entire council wore said everything I needed to know. "I see. Okay then, I'm still not just walking away from this. I have the right to address the packs, to let them know what's happening. They deserve to know and I won't run away with my tail between my legs and leave them wondering what happened. There may have been discord, but they didn't all hate me, there were those that believed in me, who followed me willingly. They have the right to know."

Seamus stood like he was about to protest, but Dax raised a hand to stop him, waving him off and sending him back into his chair.

"Fine, you may address the packs. We will inform them that you would like to address them tomorrow night. You may stay until then, we will allow you two hours to tell them what you need to say and answer questions and then, be ready to leave."

I gave them a nod, it was the best I could hope to get from them and for a moment I considered fighting it a bit harder. Then I caught the look Dax had on his face, an expression mirrored by Maxwell and Seamus and I decided that it wasn't worth it. I wouldn't be doing anyone any good if I was dead. As it was now, I could address the packs and those that hadn't heard yet could decide if they wanted to join us. Frost and I were willing to take in any that wanted to follow us, as long as they understood that this meant completely rebuilding from the bottom up.

"That's all I'm asking for. For now." Dax shot me a look that told me I'd better not ask for much more and I just smiled at him, knowing that after the next night I might have half the packs with me anyway. He was trying to keep his rear end covered and in the process, he might just be weakening his two strongest packs. I wondered if he realized that, but then decided that I wasn't about to be the one to tell him, he might just decide that I couldn't talk to the packs after all.

"We'll see you tomorrow at five then, back here."

I gave them a short, curt nod and then turned, taking Frost's hand and headed outside the building to meet up with Abbey and Austin again.

"Abbey, Austin, I need you to do something for me."

"Anything, girl, say the word." I gave my best friend and Beta a smile to thank her for being so willing to help me, no matter what I asked her to do.

"They're letting me address the packs, tomorrow evening at five. Let as many pack members as you can know. I don't trust that the council will actually tell everyone and I know there are several Rider members who will want to leave with us."

She and her father both gave me quick nods and then headed out to start knocking on doors, leaving Frost and I to drive back to our now empty house and try to get a night of sleep. We slid into the car and sat there for a few minutes, staring out into the woods at the end of the road. It was actually a nice day out considering that it was still the middle of winter and there was a blanket of pristine snow covering everything. The sun was out and the way that it shimmered off the snow on the tree branches gave the area a stunning, otherworldly golden glow. I glanced beside me at the woman sitting in the passenger seat of my car and took a good look at her as she took in the scenery.

The sunlight coming in through the windows made her hair shine a pale yellow that made her recently lightly tanned skin seem to glow. I let my gaze wander over her full lips and felt the need to run my tongue over my own. I curbed the desire to reach over and trace my fingertips down her neck, not wanting to pull her out of whatever this state was that she was in. She looked so intense, like she had something deep running through that brain of hers and I bit back the urge to ask her what she was thinking. She finally realized that I was watching her and looked over at me, the sunlight twinkling in her pale eyes and sending flickers of gold through the light purple. She took my breath away at least once a day and I hoped and prayed that she always would, something deep inside told me that she would still make me react the same way decades from now.

"What?"

The word was soft as it fell from her lips and reached my ears, leaving a shiver down my spine as it swept over me.

"Nothing, baby. Just watching you. Do you know how gorgeous you are?"

I watched her cheeks flare pink and chuckled as I started the car. I leaned over, hooked her chin with my index finger so I could turn her face back toward mine and pressed my lips to hers. I felt the moment her breath caught then heard the soft sigh as her warm breath caressed my cheek. I lingered for a few moments and then leaned away slowly, trailing my fingers through her hair as I settled back into my seat. I put the car in gear and turned it toward the house that would no longer be ours after tomorrow. Suddenly, knowing that I would have the chance to speak to the members of both packs, I didn't feel as bad about that. We could handle this, take on the challenge and move past it together, as a group. Once we left this area, the council would no longer have a say in what we did and that was a damn good feeling.

We walked in the front door of the house and I stopped to take a long look around as we entered the living room. We had put a lot of time, thought and energy into getting this house exactly like we wanted, but it was just a place. We could do the same elsewhere and I knew that we would have the chance, that we had a new home waiting for us. I could have fought harder, argued the point with the council and made a more definitive stand against their bullshit, but there didn't seem much need. They would be running their own packs into the ground and there was nothing I could really do to stop them. I knew that a good number of the members of both sides would follow Frost and I, quite a few believed in us after the things we had done the last several months. I started a little when I felt my mate's hand on my shoulder and turned to look at her, smiling.

"Come on sweetie, let's go to bed. We have a long day tomorrow and you're definitely going to need your mind bright and clear." I gave her a small nod as her hand dropped into mine and then started toward the stairs, tugging her after me. I grinned at her and the smile she shot back at me was anything but innocent and it sent my body heat through the roof in a second. I knew what that smile meant and I suddenly had something other than sleeping on my mind, as did she from the glint in those pale purple eyes.

CHAPTER TWELVE

THERE WAS a smile on my face from the moment I rolled out of bed the next morning. I was happy despite what I knew would be happening later that evening. I had one last chance to take as many of these wolves with us as possible and I planned on doing just that. We would have support in some form and we wouldn't be doing this alone, regardless of what the council wanted. I turned over and was happy to find Frost still in the bed beside me. She was up early so often these days that I couldn't remember the last time I had just been able to lay in bed and hold her in the morning. I wrapped my arms around her and pulled her in tight against me, her bare back against my equally bare chest.

"Mmmm, good morning my love." My voice was raspy and heavy with sleep, even to my own ears and all I got in response was a low grumble. "What, no good morning for me?"

"Go away, I'm not ready to be up. This damn sexy woman kept me up until all hours of the morning having her way with me."

"Oh really? I think I may be jealous, maybe I should have a talk with this woman."

I let out a soft laugh as she turned over and nuzzled her way up my neck.

"Thankfully, there's nothing for you to be jealous of, since it was you."

She brushed her nose back down the front of my throat and

then kissed the little hollow at my collarbone.

"Oh yeah, it was me, and it was *definitely* you. How do you feel this morning?"

She laughed at me and shook her head against my chest sending a flutter of tingles down over my body.

"Hmmm, how do I feel? Let me think here... I got to spend the night totally wrapped up with - and in, and around - the most gorgeous woman I've ever seen. She loved me *very* thoroughly and let me return the favor. I'd say I'm doing wonderful. How about you sweetheart, how are you feeling this morning?"

I laughed at her early morning exuberance despite her earlier protests at not wanting to be awake. I leaned in and pressed a gentle kiss to her lips then brushed her hair from her face and tucked it behind her ear.

"I feel absolutely amazing, sweetheart. I love you."

She leaned in and gave me a deeper, more intense kiss that left me breathless when she pulled away a couple minutes later.

"I love you, too."

I smirked at the breathy, barely restrained tone her voice had taken on from that one kiss and bumped her forehead gently with my own.

"Come on beautiful, time to get moving. We need to get everything loaded up before this meeting tonight so we can head right out."

She nodded and I ducked my head to brush one last kiss over the side of her neck before I rolled away and slipped from the covers. She did the same on the other side and we met at the open bag settled near the foot of the bed. We each pulled out clothes to wear for the day, got into them and then gathered our toiletries and headed for the bathroom. Once hair was done and teeth were brushed, we were ready for the day. We returned everything to the bag, zipped it up and carried it downstairs with us so we could get it loaded in the car. Everything that had been on the porch the day before had been loaded up into various vehicles, ready to be transported to our new home. I tossed the bag into our trunk and slammed it closed before we slid into the seats and got ready to go meet with our Betas.

We arrived at what would be Abbey and Kyle's home for the rest of the day and let ourselves in, finding the place still silent. We decided to make ourselves useful and raided the refrigerator for whatever we could pull together to make breakfast for our friends.

Frost had just finished making bacon and French toast as I started dumping scrambled eggs onto plates and poured coffee. After putting gallons of milk and orange juice out on the table with the plates of food we added silverware, butter and syrup just as Abbey shuffled into the room.

"Hey, hey ladies. Aren't you two just up and about with purpose this morning?" She let out a sleepy laugh as she crossed to the table and plopped down into one of the chairs. "Mmm, smells awesome, guys. Thanks."

"You are very welcome. Will Kyle be joining us?"

I grinned at my mate when she spoke, a forkful of eggs already in my mouth

"Yeah, eventually, dragging him out of bed this early is like pulling teeth, or nose hairs."

"Huh, sounds like someone else I know."

I raised an eyebrow at Frost across the table and then stuck my tongue out at her for the comment. "Real mature, sweetie."

"Dunno what you're talking about. I'm totally mature." She and Abbey glanced at each other, exchanged a look and then both burst out laughing, causing my brows to furrow down slightly. "You guys suck, I don't like either of you anymore." They knew I was full of it and both just started laughing again, which made me fling eggs at them each as Kyle walked into the room.

"Wow, food fights first thing in the morning. See what happens when I sleep in?" Abbey hopped up from her chair and jumped into her mate's arms as Frost and I grinned at them. They were so sweet together and sometimes I felt like gagging a little bit, much like I was sure they felt around us every now and then. "Well good morning to you too, honey."

Kyle's deep chuckle made us all smile as he kissed Abbey and lowered her back to the floor so they could sit at the table and enjoy breakfast. The meal went like most shared with our two best friends, chatting and making jokes like we always had. It almost felt like the day wasn't going to take a nasty turn later, like we were able to turn off the worry and anxiety for a while. Once we were finished with breakfast, we all cleaned up, which consisted of throwing the disposable dishes in the trash and washing the pans we had used.

"So, what shall we do to pass the time, kids?"

Three glares turned toward Kyle at his words and he just let out a loud laugh at us which served to make us each start giggling.

"Kids. Pfft, you're on thin ice, mister." I snapped the damp towel in my hand at him with a laugh and then hung it over the handle on the oven door. Abbey just rolled her eyes and wrapped her arms around her mate, accepting that he was one weird guy, we had all accepted that by now.

"We could make one last trip into Billings." My best friend's suggestion made me grin at her, a knowing sparkle in both our eyes.

"Arcade?"

"Arcade!" Frost and Kyle just looked at the two of us like we had grown extra heads, which made us laugh, again. "Don't ask, guys, it's kind of our thing. Go into Billings to the arcade and waste the day playing terrible video games."

"Wow, Kyle, our mates are fifteen year old boys, who knew?" I narrowed my eyes at Frost, grabbed the abandoned towel, spun it a few times then snapped it at her, the tip catching her square on her left ass cheek. "Ouch! Not nice!"

"That's what you get for calling me fifteen... And a boy! You definitely know better!"

Abbey snagged the towel from my hand as I laughed at Frost and proceeded to chase Kyle around the house with it giggling like a woman possessed. Frost and I exchanged a glance and then burst out laughing when we heard the muffled 'OUCH! That hurt!' It was shouted from the next room as Abbey apparently caught up to her mate finally.

"Got him!" The triumphant announcement came with a fist pump as Abbey walked back into the kitchen to join us. Kyle followed a few moments later, rubbing his right butt cheek and glowering at Abbey.

"Apparently. How's it feel, Kyle?" He glared at me a little then got a smirk that I really didn't care for before he snatched the towel out of Abbey's hands.

"I don't know, you tell me, oh great Alpha."

With that he started spinning the towel, I turned to run, but found Frost blocking my path. The snap a few moments later was followed immediately by a sharp little stinging sensation on my left butt cheek and I yelped a little.

"Not nice, *so* not nice!" I swiped the towel from him, balled it up and threw it on top of the refrigerator then stomped one foot. "And you!" I whirled around to face my mate with a very fake glare settled on my face that was accompanied by an evil smirk. "That wasn't very nice of you either, my love. Just wait until later, you are *so* gonna get it." She tried to look shocked and worried, but her eyes betrayed her, she knew exactly what kind of punishment was coming her way later and she was looking forward to it. I rolled my eyes at her, kissed the tip of her nose and then grabbed her hand and started for the front door. "Come on, let's get moving. We can get a few good games in before we have to come back if we go now." Kyle and Abbey followed and we all piled into Abbey's truck and headed off for the arcade in Billings to forget what the evening had in store for us.

The ride was pleasant, spent singing along to country songs, all badly as per usual, and chatting about what needed to be done once we settled on our new land. Abbey had actually managed to get everyone in the original group valid looking-passports so we could cross the northern border. Anyone who chose to leave with us at the meeting tonight would have to come up with their own on short notice or find other ways to cross the border, more wolf-shaped ways. It wasn't a terrible trip, just a few hours over the border by car, a bit shorter via four paws since one could take a direct route rather than follow the winding roads. We would be telling anyone that wanted to follow where they were headed once they made the choice that night. We weren't interested in the council knowing exactly where we were headed, even though it was well out of their reach. Being outside the council's grasp didn't mean that Greg or Daniel couldn't come and get into trouble by challenging me once we settled.

Once we reached the arcade we raced inside like a group of teenagers, the mates that had been picking on Abbey and I just a short time before now as excited as we were. We played games for several hours, even managing to turn a couple into little miniature tournaments, all of which either Abbey or I won. We were taking a bathroom break when I finally looked down at my watch and had a moment of panic. "Guys, we have to run. We have *just* enough time to make it home and get into the meeting hall before this thing starts if we pull out in the next two minutes."

We all bolted for the parking lot and into Abbey's truck then pulled back out onto the road toward Rider territory in record time. This time the ride wasn't as entertaining an affair as it had been the first go-round since we were trying to make good time. Kyle, who had driven us back, screeched to a stop outside the meeting hall and I rolled my eyes when he gave a triumphant fist pump at his total travel time before I slid out of the backseat. Once everyone was out of the truck and it was locked, we made our way inside to get the show started. My stomach was twisted into a rather nasty knot, not because I was nervous but because I knew that we could be putting into play the beginning of the end for the Rider and Clipper packs.

CHAPTER THIRTEEN

THE PACKS were just beginning to gather and if the looks on Dax and Maxwell's faces were any indication, I'd been right in not trusting them to get the word out. It appeared that they were a bit put out by the number of pack members that had shown up from both sides. I had to guess they were probably stumped as to how everyone had found out about the meeting. That eased the knot slightly since ending these two packs put the very council that had threatened my life and my future in jeopardy as well. A council with no packs to lead was worse than useless since they had all given up being pack Alphas ages ago.

I took my place at the front of the room, behind the Alpha's table that I had used at every Rider pack meeting since I had taken over. Frost took her place at my right, Abbey and Kyle at my left, Austin seated beside Frost with Rebecca at his side. We were united, a strong front for a new pack, one that I had to hope would rise up from the ashes of these that were being destroyed. At least I wouldn't have to be close enough to watch the fallout, the collapse of the packs that I had grown up in and around. That would almost be too much for me to bear if I had to be present to witness it, to watch the chaos that was sure to follow.

I knew in every fiber of my being that Greg wasn't capable to lead a troop of girl scouts much less a pack of werewolves. He would run this pack into the ground, anger members that did decide to stay behind and tough it out and I had the feeling that we would be taking in stragglers from the Rider pack for a couple years to come. The Clippers were about to be handed an even worse hand in the form of Daniel, a werewolf that believed that pain and fear were the way to keep his followers in line. I looked out over the gathered crowd for a few moments as I stood there, silently letting the last members filter in and take their seats. Once a couple minutes had passed without any new faces joining us, I took a deep breath and let it out slowly.

"Thank you all for coming tonight. I appealed to the mercy of the council to allow this meeting so that I could address you all for the last time as your Alpha."

I paused to let the rumbling murmur of whispered questions and comments flow through the gathered crowd. It was clear in that moment how many of those present knew nothing about what was happening in the packs. They had every right to know, this was no way to lead, no way to run things if one expected support from their omegas. "As some of you may already know, though I gather from the chatter that just took place, most of you don't know, I am being replaced. Both the Rider and Clipper packs will have new Alphas installed by tomorrow morning. I, Frost and my Betas, Abbey and Austin, as well as their mates, have been asked, or more to the point, ordered, to vacate the pack lands."

The chatter that went up this time forced me to take a moment and let it die down since it was more like an outcry. I hadn't actually realized how many of the Rider pack's younger members had taken to our leadership until that moment. I raised a hand to settle everyone down, noticing the expressions on the faces of the council members and feeling a bit smug at how irritated they all looked. Once the noise died down, I cleared my throat and let out a heavy sigh.

"This meeting was allowed so that I could say my goodbyes, I also intend to let those of you that would rather leave with us do just that. If you want to stay behind and help your new Alphas get settled in, we definitely understand that and wish you all luck in the coming months. For those that would like to leave with us, please find Frost or myself as soon as this meeting concludes to get directions to the new pack land and details you'll need for once you get there. For everyone else, this is more than likely the last you will see of us since, as I stated we've been asked to leave both territories permanently."

Chatter started up around the room almost instantly once I finished speaking and I caught little bits and pieces here and there. The one major theme I heard running through the chatter was questions about who would be taking over for us in the packs. I managed to get everyone quieted down and then handed the meeting off to Maxwell and Seamus so that they could fill everyone in on their new leadership. I stepped away from the Alpha's table with my little group and headed for the door, letting us out in front of the building. We were immediately surrounded by a group of people, pack members from both groups that were interested in going with us. I had to fight back the tears that threatened to break free and run loose down my cheeks at the show of support.

I managed to hold in my emotional moment until it passed and then we spent the next several minutes making sure that everyone had the information that they needed. The council was generous enough to allow those that wanted to go with us the rest of the month to pack and leave. I had to admit that I hadn't expected them to allow anyone to stay long enough to even gather their belongings, but I was sure that Dante and Brandon probably had something to do with the decision.

Once we had everyone squared away with the needed information and had marked their maps so they knew where to go, it was time to head out. We made our way back to the house to do one last round and make sure that we hadn't forgotten anything. As we stepped out onto the porch with the last box, I paused to take a look around, taking in the scenery one last time. I had come to love this house, this land and I didn't know how I was going to handle this relocation. Despite everything that had happened over the last year or so, all the changes that we had gone through, I was actually no good with change. I had held it together and managed to get through thanks to the support system I had in place, the same system I knew would get me through this change. It would be my family, my mother, brothers, Frost, Abbey and her parents and even Kyle that would get me through all of this.

I was turning to take one last look at the house we had made our own, the place that had been home for what had turned out to be such a short time when I caught sight of someone approaching the porch. I handed the box I was holding off to Frost and made my way down the stairs to meet our last minute guest, shocked to find that it was August. I had recently made him an Enforcer in the Rider pack despite the fact that he had just turned seventeen a few months earlier. He looked heartbroken and I had an idea why, his parents hadn't ever truly supported Frost and I assuming leadership of the pack. I had to assume that they had decided to stay and follow Greg as their new Alpha which wouldn't bode well for poor August. He had confided in us a few weeks after our return from California, telling us that he was gay and that he was terrified to tell his parents. As far as I knew, he still hadn't told them.

I stopped at the bottom of the stairs as he ran the last few yards and threw himself into my arms, sobbing. I was at a loss for what to do for him and I glanced back at Frost for help, unsure what to say or do to ease his pain. She set the box down on the porch and came down the steps to join us, giving me a sad smile as she rubbed his back. It had to be an odd sight since August was only about a year and a half younger than we were and a rather large kid at six feet tall and was built like a brick wall. He dwarfed me and yet here he was, bent over, head on my shoulder, crying like a little kid.

"Hey, come on, try to calm down a little and talk to us, August. We can't help you if we don't know what's wrong, sweetie."

Frost was calm and collected, the voice of reason and support, just like always.

"I can't stay here, I just can't. Greg found out about me and I just know he's gonna make my life hell. I have to tell my parents, they need to know."

I nodded a little bit as he leaned back, having figured it would happen eventually. Greg was just as narrow minded as my father had been. I wouldn't be surprised in the least if he made life hard on the poor kid. I reached up and wiped the tears from his cheeks, brushing his shaggy black hair behind his ear, he really needed a haircut.

"Will you come with me before you leave? Help me tell them?"

"Of course we will. Come on, let's go."

I smiled at Frost when she answered for us both without hesitation then reached over and took my hand. The smile that took over August's face made it to his eyes and even though they were still brimming with tears there was a sparkle in them you couldn't miss from a mile off. We made our way to his house, ready to support him as he told his parents, to do whatever needed to be done no matter what their reaction. When we reached the house, he made his way up the steps and across the porch with us on his heels and then, after a short pause to gather himself, walked inside.

"Mom? Dad? Are you here? I need to talk to you."

"In the living room."

His mother's reply came from off to our left and we followed him into the other room, pausing to take in the group seated there. I recognized them all, his parents, Sadie and Michael as well as his two older brothers Tim and Forrest, and they were also joined by several other Rider pack members. The group looked our direction and the expressions we received were not friendly in the least, downright caustic from Michael and Forrest.

"What are they doing in my house?"

His father rose from his chair as he spoke, obviously not happy with Frost and I being present in his living room.

"They're here because I asked them to come with me. I have something that I need to tell you and I need them here for support."

"What kind of support could they possibly offer you? We're your family, just talk to us."

Tim's words made him pause to take a deep breath and hazard a glance back at us, getting two nods and smiles in return.

"Before they left, I wanted to tell you all that, well, I'm like them." The confused looks he got from those present told us that they didn't understand what he meant and he would have to elaborate a bit for them. "Mom, dad, I'm gay."

I heard a gasp from his mother a second before the glass she had been holding hit the wood floor and shattered. I chanced a quick look in her direction and found her hand covering her mouth before my eyes swept to his father. Michael looked positively livid and at the first twitch of a muscle from the older male I had dropped Frost's hand and was between the massive man and his son in a second.

"Get out of my way!"

I stood my ground as he shouted in my face and calmly shook my head at him, not about to let him take out his anger on poor August.

"No."

"You have no right to get in the middle of this, you little bitch, now move!"

"You'll have to make me, but I don't think you can so you might as well settle down."

"Don't you dare walk into my home and tell me to settle down. You aren't even supposed to be here! Get out! As for you..." His anger turned toward August who stood his ground despite the nervous energy I could feel rolling off of him. He was one tough kid, and brave, if not a little headstrong and stupid sometimes, definitely impulsive. "You will take that back, you will come sit down with your family, enjoy dinner and then tomorrow you will meet Alina as promised."

"No, I won't. I refuse. I don't want to meet her, I'm sure she's a great girl, but dad, I don't want a mate, not now, and if I did, it would be another male."

That only seemed to stoke the bigger man's anger further and I felt the growl ripple out from him, it made my skin crawl a little.

"Get out. I want you out of my house. You want to be like these two? Sick and twisted, living this disgusting and perverted lifestyle? Fine, then hope they'll take you with them because you no longer live here."

"Come on August, let's go get your things, you're leaving with us tonight."

Frost's soft voice brought a smile to my face as she said exactly what had been on my mind. I stood my ground as she went upstairs to help him gather the few belongings he wanted to take with him. Thankfully, one of those happened to be a very real passport he had obtained for a trip overseas his family had taken the year before. Once they returned, we gathered up the bags they had packed for him, four suitcases, two duffel bags and a backpack in all, and headed for the front door.

"I hope you're prepared to deal with him, you little bitch, because he had better not come crawling back here. He no longer has a family."

I dropped the two suitcases I was carrying, turned on my heel and took the few strides back to where Michael was standing, getting right up in his face.

"Yes, he does. He always has, and it was never any of you. So go fuck yourself."

My voice was steady as I spoke and once I was finished a smile crossed my face as I lowered myself down off my tip-toes and turned to rejoin August and my mate by the door. They were both beaming at me and I felt a little swell of pride in the moment as we left the house, August and his baggage in tow. It was time for all of us to start over, begin a new life somewhere that we would be accepted and loved for who, and what, we were.

CHAPTER FOURTEEN

WE DIDN'T go far that first night, we still needed to get some kind of sleep if we were planning on settling in properly when we reached our destination. We stopped and spent the night in Great Falls, the entire troupe pulling into a truck stop intent on catching whatever rest that we could. All told we had a large group that had left with us immediately, Frost and I were in a truck that we had rented for the occasion with the car on a trailer behind it and had August in tow. Abbey and Kyle had piled all of their junk into Abbey's truck and a U-Haul trailer they were towing along. Austin and Rebecca were towing their car behind the RV they had bought a couple years earlier. They were followed by a converted school bus that Dante had bought and worked on for travels after his son was born. It held he, his mate and son as well as Shane and my mother and was trailed by Brandon's truck, Tristan stretched out in the backseat asleep.

There were a few families from both packs that had gotten wind of what was happening and had packed up, prepared to leave with us the moment we pulled out. Our final number was twenty-two adults, five youths between thirteen and seventeen and ten children under twelve. It was a good sized group to be leaving with and we had managed to take some of the stronger members of both packs, though not all. We were thankful to have so many to help us resettle and start over, but we knew that we had challenges ahead of us. Thankfully, I had taken Austin's advice when I started working and saved almost everything, not to mention that I rarely spent my allowance, birthday or Christmas money or anything I got for other holidays. Add to that the money Frost had saved and what her grandparents had left her when they died along with what those that were leaving with us had stashed away and we had pulled together enough to buy some land and make the trip.

We had been in touch with the owner of a stretch of open land for sale over the border in Alberta and had already set the purchase in motion. We would complete the paperwork once we arrived and then get started on renovating the older houses that were on the property already. We would make the living space available to us work until we could build more housing. We would just have to hope that those individuals that followed us wouldn't end up regretting the choice a few months down the line. We pulled in behind the truck stop, found space for all the vehicles and settled in for the night. Once I checked on everyone to make sure that those in the party had everything that they needed for the night and got August settled into the RV with Austin and Becca, I climbed back into the rented truck. Frost and I slipped into the backseat and crawled under the blankets we had packed before she cuddled up against me. Within moments her breathing evened out and her heart rate slowed, telling me she had fallen asleep.

I laid in the dark, staring out the window above my feet and thinking about everything that had happened that had led us to this point, again. No matter what had happened, I couldn't bring myself to feel bad about any of the steps that I had taken. We were in the middle of a transition that would be hard on everyone involved, but the choices had been made with my eyes wide open. We had left a lot of people behind from both packs, but I couldn't bring myself to feel bad for any of them. They had chosen to stay where they were, to weather out the coming storms and fall into line behind what was sure to be terrible leadership. I hated the idea of the packs we had grown up in falling apart, but they were no longer our concern and we had to move on, move forward. I drifted off to sleep with a smile on my face at the idea, moving forward, it sounded like just the thing to help this new pack bond and become a family.

The next morning we all piled into the diner attached to the truck stop to get some breakfast before setting out again. We still had a hike ahead of us before we reached our destination and I wasn't crazy enough to believe that the GPS estimate of fourteen hours was very accurate. Maybe two people, in a single vehicle, not towing small children and without a border crossing, but this was bound to take a while once you factored in all those things. The beginning of the meal was silent, most of the members of the rag-tag group still working on waking up. Once the first small hints of chatter began, though, the group seemed to come alive and they were all soon talking and laughing together. It was almost like none of the terrible events of the last few weeks had gotten any of them down, but I knew better. We had all been impacted in one way or another, we were just healing, coming together and working through it. That was all that mattered and it was what would get us all through everything in the end.

With breakfast finished and everyone reloaded into vehicles, we set out once more with every intention of making it across the border and to a decent place to eat by dinner time. Frost and I chatted with August as we drove, getting to know him a little better and finding that he was a rather funny guy once he wasn't worried about everything. We laughed, sang along with the stereo and snacked as we followed the highway out of the only home any of us had ever known. It was all at once terrifying and exciting and I found that I couldn't wait to get to our destination and get settled in. We were making decent time, but I knew that the biggest hold up might be getting through border patrol with so many people.

At least we had already started the process of buying land on the other side, that paperwork would help. There was also the fact that many of the old Clipper pack members had held jobs outside pack lands in various fields and had managed to secure jobs on the other side. We were fairly certain that we would get through without any objections, after being thoroughly searched for contraband, of course. What should have only been a two hour drive or so to the border ended up taking almost five as two of the younger children in the group seemed to come down with some strange, sudden onset youth incontinence. After stopping half a dozen times for the kids to relieve themselves, which was wearing my patience a little thin, as well as stopping for lunch, we finally reached the border.

The inspections of the vehicles and their contents took a while, as we had expected. The questions we were asked weren't that difficult to answer and the responses that we gave were completely honest. The paperwork, however, was what made my heart rate kick into overdrive. We waited as it was inspected and hoped that the forged documents, which constituted much of the stack, would pass muster. I was tied in knots as we waited for the men to get through it all. When we were finally allowed through, I released a ragged sigh I hadn't realized I'd been holding. This was a stressful trip and I was hoping that we could settle in for a day or two before having to do any major work once we arrived.

As it was, our arrival proved that resting wouldn't be on the agenda for a while. We had our work cut out for us. The land was amazing, the views stunning despite the chill in the air and the snow covering the ground. The houses perched in the middle of the expanse of about one hundred acres we had worked out buying were in decent shape, but in need of some TLC and updating. I let out a sigh as I hopped from the truck and took in the house in front of me, the one that would be my new home with Frost. It was a cute little thing, roughly ranch in style, single story with a covered porch along the front that wrapped around the left side. It was desperately in need of some fresh paint, or siding, or something to make it look less... Sad. Could houses look sad? This one did somehow and I could only shake my head at the poor thing. We had met the woman we were buying the acreage from at the property line upon our arrival and finished the last remaining paperwork.

It had been lucky for us that we had come across a woman working in the real estate office we had contacted that was of our kind. She was a werewolf who knew of this stretch of land we were standing on and that it had belonged to another pack, one that had relocated when they needed more space. The former owners, the pack Alphas, had agreed to sell us the land for a bargain that we really couldn't pass up. It was perfect for a new pack that was just starting out, but looked like the old pack had been gone for at least half a decade, maybe more. I looked down at the several sets of keys settled in my palm and just smiled. It wasn't much, but it was a place to start, and it was ours. That was all that mattered. I tossed the keys a little, catching them again and then made my way up to the main house, Frost on my heels. I wanted to see what we were working with inside the home, how much space we had and how much cleaning and remodeling we would be stuck with.

I expected the lock to put up more of a struggle than it did, surprised at the ease with which the bolt turned. I eased the door open and was amazed to find that, while the outside of the place looked like no one had cared in years, the inside was clean and actually more updated than I had expected. The deep, cherry-colored wood flooring of the entryway and living room beyond shone like they had recently been polished, the walls seemed to bear a fresh coat of paint as well, a light, creamy off-white color. The fireplace settled in the corner of the living room was surrounded in river rock with an absolutely gorgeous granite hearth. I stepped further into the space, allowing Frost in behind me and heard her gasp as she took in what I was seeing.

I walked across the reasonably-sized living room and into the kitchen, finding pristine ceramic tile the color of mountain ice on the floors, almost white with just a hint of pale blue. The cabinets were a deep color bordering somewhere between cherry and chocolate, the countertops the same coloring as the floor, but in a stunning flash of granite. The appliances were stainless steel and looked somewhat new, definitely only slightly used. I continued through the house, marveling at each new room that we came upon in a bit of disbelief. Most of the house carried the same wood as the entry and living room except for the bathrooms, which held the same color combination as the kitchen.

There were six bedrooms and four and a half bathrooms in the house total. I was floored with the luck we had met with. I stepped out the sliding glass door on the back of the house, expecting to find a snow covered expanse of land in the back and was met with an enclosed pool room. The pool itself had been drained and stood completely empty, but I could tell it sported a deep end of at least ten or twelve feet and a hot tub attached. I was stunned and couldn't speak as I stood there and stared at it, the world around me completely tuned out.

"Pick your jaw up off the floor and say something would ya, lass?"

I jumped a little at the first sound of the voice, but then the familiar accent washed over me and I whirled around to see Hank standing there smiling at me, Barkley at his side.

"I, what? What are you two doing here?"

They glanced at each other and then back to me before bursting out laughing, probably at the look on my face.

"Honey, my brother's pack used to own this land. His Alpha heard the people interested in buying were pack from the US and wanted to some information. Turned out, it's a small world and we had all the information he needed. He made sure, after we explained the situation, that he sent some of his guys out here to get these places fixed up a little for you. They still need work, but it's nothing you can't handle I'm sure."

I didn't know what to say so I just stood there, silent and completely in awe of what our friends had made happen for us.

"Now before you go getting all weepy on us, they aren't all finished like this. He managed to get five of the eight done for ya, but the rest, you're on your own with. Well, not completely, we'll stay a bit and help out with the heavy lifting."

The grin on Hank's face finally made me pull my jaw up off the floor and laugh. We had been through so much and knowing that we had someone, anyone, on our side in all of this meant the world to me.

"Thank you, both of you. This means a lot. How much trouble did you get in because of helping us?"

I was terrified to ask, but I had to know, the fact that the two Alphas were here, in Canada, alone, probably wasn't a good sign. Had they lost their pack as well? I wasn't sure that I could live with myself if that was the case.

"None at all." I turned my gaze on Barkley and gave him a look that rather clearly told him that I didn't believe him one bit. "Honestly, Kyndle, no harm done. Our council is a little more, let's say, progressive, than your former council was. They would have to be with us as Alphas, wouldn't they? Point is that we didn't get in trouble for helping you, what we got was a pat on the back and several high fives for it."

I was stunned, I had known that the councils in the various parts of the country were very different, but I hadn't realized how different. Maybe we should have just headed into California rather than fleeing the country. Then again, now that we had seen the land and this house, we had made the right choice as far as I was concerned. All I could do once it all sank in was shake my head and let out a small chuckle as Frost slipped her arm around my waist, a smile firmly on her face.

"Well, thank you, for everything. We'll never be able to repay you for everything you've done for us."

Hank waved me off with the brush of one massive hand and let out a small huff of air.

"Don't even start, girlie. Look, just knowing that you're safe, will be settled and aren't alone is enough thanks for us."

Barkley's smile told me that he agreed completely and my heart swelled at the show of support from our friends, friends we hadn't even known a year ago. It was weird how the world worked out sometimes, we were just lucky that it had worked out in our favor this time.

"Well, fine, I won't mention it again. Frost, let's go walk through the other houses and get everyone settled in. We'll figure out what we're doing from there." She gave me a nod and then we each hugged Hank and Barkley on our way past them toward the front of the house. We stepped out onto the porch to discover that everyone had unloaded themselves from their vehicles and were milling around chatting. "Okay everyone, Frost and I will be taking this house here, probably with a few people staying with us thanks to the size of it. We're about to go check out the rest and figure out who will fit where for the time being. Once we finish the walk through, we'll let you all know. For now, Dante, why don't you and Brandon set up the grills and get some food going, I'm sure everyone is starving by now."

My brothers gave each other a smile that I swear was reserved just for men when grilling was mentioned and then set to work. I shook my head at them, rolled my eyes and started for the next house with a smile on my face. After walking through the rest of the houses on the property, Frost and I settled in at the small card table Dante had set up in our new dining room and set to work. We had to fit thirty seven people into five houses, which sported a combined total of twenty rooms. The last three houses that hadn't been remodeled yet weren't currently in livable condition and cut nine bedrooms out of the equation for us. We spent the next several minutes arranging, rearranging and shuffling before we finally decided where everyone would be.

The task complete and everyone with a place to sleep, we had filled all twenty usable rooms, but had managed to keep families together and just needed to get some furniture into the rooms. After unloading everything that we had brought with us we decided to just settle into sleeping bags for the night and get everything furnished the next day. We all needed some sleep before we made the trek into the nearest town and dealt with hauling and building furniture.

CHAPTER FIFTEEN

AFTER A somewhat awkward night of sleep since wood floors with only sleeping bags for padding were not comfortable, we got moving, had breakfast and started splitting everyone up. After the task of convincing those we wanted to hang back to stay, we started out, leaving half the new pack in charge of the kids we'd brought with us, the rest of us, including Frost, Abbey, Kyle and I, headed into the nearest town to buy some furniture. With some help from Barkley and Hank we managed to get everything purchased and loaded then set back out toward our new home. Home. It had been such a fleeting thing the last year that I was almost scared to even think it for fear that it might vanish like the dream I kept feeling it was. I pushed the thought aside, not wanting to let those doubts creep in when we had so much to do.

We were all going to be busy over the next several weeks and I was honestly just thankful that we had a handful of teachers and tutors among our adult followers. The children needed to stay up to date on their studies until we could find a school to get them all enrolled in. We reached our new pack territory just around dinner time, unloaded and decided to eat before setting to the task of furniture building. We handed out the furniture to those that would be using it, letting them, or in the case of the younger kids, their parents, assemble it all. As it managed to work out, our second night on our new land was spent in actual beds, something my back was thankful for. The next two days were spent just taking a break, needing some time to relax after the turmoil we had left and then the trip we'd made.

We knew that we needed to get to work if we expected to make any progress on the three houses that still looked as abandoned as they had been. The five in use needed new exterior paint as well as some work on the porches and railings, but they were acceptable for the moment. Hours of bonfires, roasting hot dogs and marshmallows and laughing together like we hadn't just been through hell and come out the other side did each of us a world of good. We let the work wait, knowing that it would still be there two or three weeks later and knowing that our new pack needed the time to recuperate.

By the time we set to work on the last of the houses, we were all in much better spirits and I for one felt like I could take on the world. Frost pointed out that I already had in my own way and I just hugged her for the sentiment. The living situations were manageable, but we definitely needed to get those other three houses ready to be lived in. We also knew that we would need a few more started before we had more members showing up to settle in. There was no way we would be able to fit everyone who had expressed the desire to follow us into the spaces we had available.

As for Frost and I, we had a full house for the moment, the two of us in the master bedroom, Abbey and Kyle in another, Austin and Rebecca taking up a third, Dante and his mate Sharon in a fourth while their son Carter took up a fifth. The last room in the main house, which was actually the second room by size, only slightly smaller than the master room itself, housed four of our teens. We had decided to room August with the three girls that had come with us, Melissa, Simone and Lydia. There had been some apprehension on the parts of the girls' families at first but once they got to know August and realized that he wasn't a threat to their girls, they eased up. The four of them, as Frost and I had hoped, had become inseparable. We continually had to knock on their door in the middle of the night to stop the giggling going on in the room and make them sleep.

Barkley and Hank stayed long enough to help us get one of the remaining three houses in decent shape, but then had to head back to their pack. We thanked them for all their help, extending an open invitation to visit whenever they wanted before sending them on their way. It had been great to see them again and the help that they had provided had been a godsend in the last several days. Working on the houses was proving slow since we often had doors and windows standing open and the winter chill settled anywhere and everywhere it could. Frequent breaks to huddle by the fire we always had going and warm up broke up our progress daily. It was moving forward though, and by our own hands which was something that we couldn't have been more happy about, or proud of. We knew that it would all come together and we would be a bit more settled by the time spring came around. That was more than we could have hoped for when all of this began so many months ago.

It was in the middle of the fourth week since settling on the new land that an old pickup truck wound its way up the long, muddy road to the main house. I set down the mug I was holding and tugged my boots on before I stepped out onto the front porch of our new house. I narrowed my eyes at the vehicle, trying to place the dark green exterior, rust showing through the paint here and there. As it drew closer, the memory suddenly settled in my mind and I pulled the long sleeved over shirt I was wearing tighter around myself and watched the approach. I headed toward the steps that would lead me off the porch and down to the curved road that served as our driveway just as the truck came to a stop and grinned a little. The door creaked open and the driver hopped out, slammed it closed again and came around toward the house. "Hey stranger." A startled yelp came from the small woman before she turned deep brown eyes my direction, a glare in place until she realized who had spoken.

I watched the expression on her face change and smiled back at her as she let out the most feminine squeal I had ever heard and launched herself at me. I let go of my over shirt and got my arms out of the way just before she slammed into me, knocking us both into the snow. The commotion brought Frost outside to see what was going on and the giggling coming from the snow at the bottom of the stairs drew her gaze to where we were laying. I knew how it must look, her mate on her back in the snow, an adorable blonde with dark, chocolate eyes and curves most women would kill for straddling her and holding her in a death grip. A normal, or lesser woman might have freaked out, started yelling and even thrown accusations around. Frost was not a normal woman however, and was definitely not lesser and she just rolled her eyes, crossed her arms over her chest and leaned her shoulder against the pillar holding up the awning over the porch. She was waiting for an explanation and as soon as I got Celeste the hell off of me, she would get one.

"Celeste! Jesus, woman, get off me! I'm freezing my ass off down here!"

I was laughing as the words left my mouth and she seemed to realize that I was practically covered in snow while only wearing pajama pants, a tee shirt and a thin flannel over-shirt.

"Oh shit! Sorry!"

She jumped up suddenly and offered me her hand, helping me up out of the snow and then lending a hand in getting the snow brushed off.

"What the hell are you doing here?"

I pulled the shirt tight around me again as I studied her, wondering what on earth had brought her all the way up to our land, and how she had found me in the first place.

"Well, I got wind of what happened. Figured I'd come find you, see how much was true." I grinned and shook my head as I studied her standing there in front of me. She was shorter than me at only five foot two and was absolutely adorable if I was being honest. Shoulder length dirty blonde hair framed a soft face that looked a lot younger than her eighteen years. Matching eyebrows nestled in perfectly sculpted arches above those big, expressive, dark chocolate eyes I had known almost my entire life. She was built smaller than I was, her frame more feminine, more like Frost's and Abbey's than my more tomboyish build. The girl was probably lucky if she hit a hundred and ten pounds soaking wet wearing wool, she was just tiny, yet those curves still managed to be firmly in place. I'd always found her more cute than anything, but having not seen her in nearly three years, I was amazed at how mature she looked now.

"Well, come on in and I'll fill you in." I nodded toward the front door and then turned to head up the steps, Frost already slipping through the door as we started onto the porch. We slipped into the house and I closed the door firmly behind Celeste, shivering as I stripped off the now soaked flannel. I tossed the now useless shirt over the back of the couch we had put in the living room. Frost was adding a couple logs to the fireplace in the corner, her pale blonde hair pulled over one shoulder. I watched her for a moment with a smile before I crossed the room as she stood and wrapped my arms around her waist. She leaned back against me as I brushed my lips up the side of her neck, eliciting a soft sigh as her head dropped back gently onto my shoulder. "Love you." The whispered words made a grin tweak up her lips which made mine respond in kind. A small giggle from behind us made me look over my shoulder at Celeste and throw a mock glare at her.

"Well, looks like that rumor was true at least." The grin she was giving us made me roll my eyes and I turned back, dropped a light kiss on Frost's lips and then went to move away. She stopped me for a moment with a hand on my arm, her 'love you too' whispered against my lips before she kissed me back just as lightly then released my arm again. "Oh gods, must you be so disgustingly sweet. I'm gonna barf over here."

"Real mature, Celeste. Come on in, make yourself at home." I watched as she dropped herself into one of our new chairs and then Frost and I settled onto the couch. I sat against one end and then she settled herself in against me, her legs stretched out on the length of the couch. "So, first off, Celeste, this is my mate, Frost. Baby, this is Celeste."

They seemed to take a moment and regard each other and then each nodded and returned focus to me. I didn't miss the expression that flickered across Celeste's face for a brief moment and I was sure Frost hadn't either. Somehow that momentary look told me that her light hearted banter with us was covering something else, something not nearly as sweet and innocent. I knew I was going to have to give Frost a bit more than just her name after what she had seen out front but that could wait. "So what other rumors did you hear?"

"Your father tried to mate you off to some asshat dude against your wishes."

"True."

"Damn, okay. Then, you ran off, disappeared for months."

"Also true. Decided to take a trip to California."

"That's kinda awesome. Okay, ummm, you beat the shit outta formerly mentioned asshat."

"True, though I actually killed him. He challenged me and I won."

"I always knew you were a badass under all that adorable you had going on." That comment, along with the grin and wink that followed it, tugged one of Frost's pale brows up slightly and I knew I was in for questioning again later. "Alright, let's see, you got yourself bonded to another female, which I see was true."

"Yep, very true. The asshat was her brother."

"Well now, that's a tidbit I didn't hear. Nice. Anyway, you went back home and took over his pack."

"Yep."

"Then your dad flipped his shit, went all angry postal worker on you and you killed him."

"Right on the nose."

"Then the council decided to be douchebags, as they're prone to be, and booted you. So you ran, to Canada." All I could do was nod at her with a small chuckle at her assessment of the council, she'd hit that nail right on the head. "Okay, so I'm all caught up. Mostly anyway, though I do have a few more personal questions. Those can wait until later though." I felt one eyebrow arc up at her and she just flashed me a grin that I knew all too well, I hated that grin, it meant that she was going to be a royal pain in my ass later. "For the moment, it was a long damn drive alone and I feel like I haven't showered in a week. You mind?"

"Not at all, there's a room at the end of the hall right there, has a bathroom next to it. Feel free to use it, and the room is yours if you need to rest." I felt a small sigh from the woman in my arms and as Celeste flashed me a grin and hopped up to head out to her truck, I assumed to get her belongings. A moment later Frost stood as well. The rooms of our house were slowly emptying as we finished the other houses so we had two now available for sudden houseguests. I had the feeling from that sigh that Frost wasn't sure this guest was someone she wanted around. "You okay?"

"Fine. Just tired, I think I need a nap." I watched her walk down the hallway and if I knew my mate at all, she was far from fine. I knew that while she had reacted well to the initial scene, what had just taken place had shaken her and I needed to explain. I heard our bedroom door click closed and was just about to follow her when Celeste walked back into the house, a single suitcase in tow.

"Ball and chain decided to give you some space, huh? Guess she knows you pretty well. Come on, my shower can wait, I wanna talk while we have a minute." I was about to protest, but before I had the chance Celeste had grabbed my arm and was dragging me back toward the door. I grabbed my jacket as we passed the coat rack and tugged it on just as the blast of cold hit me when she pulled the door open. We stepped out onto the front porch and when she dropped my arm, I just pulled the door closed and followed her over to the swing we had put up the week before. She dropped herself onto it and I just stood there for a moment and stared at her. If I knew Celeste, and I knew her better than I cared to admit, she was up to something. "Come on, sit, I don't bite." I narrowed my eyes at the comment and she let out a giggle, covering her mouth with her hand to cut it off abruptly. "Okay, maybe I do but, seriously, Kyn, come sit."

I winced a little at the old nickname and the ease with which she still used it and moved to sit beside her, still not sure I really should. "I'm willing to talk, Celeste, but only talk." The look of shock that she gave me at my comment was as fake as her trimmed, acrylic nails and I glowered at her a little.

"Okay fine, I got it, only talking. Honestly though, Kyndle, this is all crazy. I knew you had a thing for this girl, but I mean, come on, those summers, it didn't seem this serious."

"Of course it was serious, it was always serious, Celeste!" I had raised my voice at her without really meaning to do so, but I hated the parts of my past her appearance was dredging up. I was trying to forget some past summers and I didn't want to have to explain them to anyone, definitely not Frost.

"Whoa! Settle down, no need to bite my head off! All I'm saying is that, if it was serious, if you were serious, what was this?" I looked at her hand as she gestured between the two of us and my gut clenched as I tried to breathe normally. "What was I?" I was trying to concentrate, inhale, exhale, inhale, exhale, don't look up, don't think about it. I knew I should brush off the question, get up and walk away, go talk to Frost, but I couldn't make my legs move. What was worse was that I knew that Frost, thanks to our heightened hearing, was probably catching every word of this conversation.

"What do you want me to say, Celeste? I don't know how to answer that."

I finally looked up at her, my blue eyes meeting her brown ones and I saw something flicker behind them for a moment, something like pain. I hated the thought of hurting her but I didn't know what she expected of me after all this time. Three years and six weeks had passed since the last time I had seen Celeste and it had been a heated parting, a fight that had kept me from returning after that summer when I was fifteen.

"Nothing, I guess. I should have learned not to expect anything from you, Kyndle. I told you when this started that you'd break my heart. Do you remember what you told me? Do you?" I shook my head and looked away again, not because I didn't remember, but because I wished I could forget. "You promised me that I wouldn't end up just some mistake you regretted. That you wouldn't leave me broken and alone, but you did. You got me all wrapped up in this whirlwind, made me fall in love with you and then just cut me out, forgot about me and moved right on with your life. I hope you're enjoying it. I'll get my things and stay in town."

I felt her stand up from the swing and then heard the front door open and close again, but I was frozen in place, unable to move. My heightened senses were allowing me to hear something that made my heart tighten, the soft sniffles coming from the master bedroom, from Frost, she had heard everything. I had to talk to her, tell her everything and make it right again, I hated that I had hurt her.

CHAPTER SIXTEEN

I STOOD up and walked into the house once Celeste had left again, turning down the hall on the left that led away from the living room and toward our bedroom. I paused outside the door and took a deep breath before I pushed it open and stepped inside. I closed it behind me and looked at the bed, the sight made the heart that had been tight in my chest break. My sweet mate was lying on our bed, curled into herself, clutching one of my pillows, sobbing into it. I kicked my boots off, dropped my jacket to the floor and crossed to the bed. I crawled up beside her and wrapped my arms around her, half expecting her to push me away, to be angry, to yell at me and want me to leave.

None of those things happened and instead she simply lay there, crying, like I wasn't there at all. I wasn't really sure which was worse, but I felt like my world was in chaos yet again. Why couldn't I catch a break? I waited while she cried it out and then felt my stomach knot when she pushed away and slid to the other side of the bed. She sat up and I followed suit, watching her back as she stared out the window.

"Baby."

I reached out for her as I whispered the single word, hoping that she would give me the chance to explain myself.

"Don't, Kyndle." The rebuff made me recoil a little as she stood up and walked around the bed, her arms wrapped around her own body as if she was protecting herself, from me. She stopped in the middle of the room and turned to face me, the redness of her eyes making my already broken heart ache. "Talk, and this better be good."

"Frost, I've known Celeste since I was about five. Do you remember those trips I told you about that we used to take every summer, the ones out to my Uncle Brian's place in Wyoming?" I watched as she nodded, studying me hard, making sure that I wasn't lying to her. I suddenly felt glad that I was going to be able to tell her all of this myself before this mental link was complete and she got it all from my memories. "Baby, Brian isn't really my Uncle. He, Dane, and Austin all grew up together. Dane and Austin stayed with the Clipper pack and Brian left, he wanted his own pack, wanted to be Alpha. He found a small pack in Wyoming with an older Alpha that didn't have any children. The old guy took him in and handed him the pack. Celeste is his daughter." I saw her eyes narrow a bit, watched as she processed and then caught her slight nod, telling me to continue.

"The summer after I turned twelve, we went for our yearly visit and, as usual, Celeste and I spent all our time together. I have four brothers, she has five, we needed to get away from them during those trips so, we ended up spending that time off together. That summer, everything... Everything changed between us. She kissed me, I let her. I already knew I liked girls. I mean you had already started going to school with us at that point and even if I'd been in denial before that, well... Anyway, I had no idea she felt the same though and, it was new and exciting and I finally had someone that knew about me, that felt the way I did.

"We spent that summer, and then the next two, vanishing together during the day for the couple months my family was there. I was young and it was exciting and I didn't know that I would ever have any chance with you. So I promised her things I never should have, things I had no right promising her, or anyone back then." My eyes were pleading with her to understand that I had just been a kid, getting caught up in the moment, in a summer fling, but she looked away from me, her eyes meeting the carpet. She seemed to fold in on herself, her grip around her own torso tightening a little as I watched her fight back more tears.

"How far did it go?"

"No further than what I told you. We kissed, we held hands, but it was never more than that."

"Kyndle," she whispered my name harshly as she looked up and finally met my eyes again, I knew what she was about to ask me, I would answer her honestly because I had nothing to lie about. "Did you love her? Do you love her?"

"No." Our eyes stayed locked as she searched mine for the truth in that single word, obviously finding it as she let out a ragged sigh and took the few steps toward the bed. I slipped off the edge and wrapped my arms around her as she reached me, holding her as she held onto me right back. It felt like she was hanging on for dear life, like she was terrified that I would change my mind and walk out and my heart broke all over again. "I'm so sorry, Frost. I should have told you ages ago. I never thought I'd see her again to be honest. That last summer, I was fifteen, you and I had finally started spending time together as friends and I just knew, even then I could feel it." I shifted my weight and leaned her back a bit so I could look into those beautiful eyes.

"I knew you were the one, that I needed to do whatever it took to be with you. That meant cutting her off before things went any further. She was furious with me, we had a fight and I never went back to visit again. I was hoping that her showing up here today meant that she had gotten over it, that she had moved on and we could go back to being friends again. It would appear that I was off in that assumption. I'm sorry baby, I never meant to hurt you, I swear." I didn't get to say anything else after that since she gripped my shirt, pulled me in and let her lips meet mine. The contact sent a shiver through me, a ripple of recognition that I had almost screwed everything up, that my own denial could have very easily cost me the woman I loved more than anything in the world. I knew that I would need to sit down, rake through my own memories and pull up everything I could remember, tell her every last detail that I could recall. I couldn't let this happen ever again, she deserved better. She pulled away after a few long moments and then nuzzled her face into the side of my neck.

"You should know by now that you can tell me anything. I don't ever want to feel like this again, Kyndle."

I wondered how many times a heart could break as she whispered the words against my neck, her warm breath leaving a ripple of goose-bumps in its wake.

"I know sweetheart. I swear I'll dig through every damn memory I have and tell you everything. I hate that I made you feel this way."

"What are you going to do if she comes back?" I exhaled heavily as I thought about that, wondering the same thing. It wasn't a matter of if she came back to talk to me again, it was a matter of when. Celeste was never one to give up when something was in her sights and I knew she came here for a reason. She had tracked me down because she wanted something and I was terrified of finding out what it could be.

"When she comes back, because believe me, love, she will, we'll handle it."

"We'll handle it? Both of us?"

"Yes, both of us, baby. She needs to get it through her head that I'm taken and whatever might have existed between us in her head was just that, in her head. It's been over for years and I have no intention of revisiting it. I'm right where I'm meant to be."

That brought out the smile I loved so much and, in that moment, my heart began to mend a little. A shrill ring cut through the room and it took a moment to remember that it was our phone. We had all had land lines connected since we had settled in, but I still wasn't used to them. Frost leaned over and picked the handset up out of its cradle before she pressed the button to answer it and held it to her ear.

"Hello? Oh hey Abbey... Yeah, come on over. I think we need to tell you this in person... Yep, bring them along... Okay, see you in a few minutes." She ended the call and tossed the phone on the bed before looking at me with a small smile. "Abbey, Kyle, Austin and Becca are headed over. They saw the truck out front and wanted to know what was going on." I gave her a nod and then looked down at us, both still in our pajamas and I laughed a little.

"We should probably put some actual clothes on and make some coffee or something."

The smile that settled on her face told me that she agreed and we slipped into the closet to change into jeans and tee shirts. We were just wandering into the living room to check the fire when there was a knock on the door. Frost moved toward the kitchen to start coffee while I let our friends into the house. We had managed to do enough shuffling that Abbey, Austin, Frost and I were spread through the small collection of houses. We had wanted to make sure that one of the four of us was always close for the members of our new pack so I had moved my Betas and their mates into other houses. I popped the door and waved our friends in, and then moved to toss another log onto the fire, making sure that it was going strong. Frost came in a couple minutes later with a tray that held a carafe of coffee, creamer, sugar and enough mugs for everyone.

She got everyone settled with coffee and then the two of us snuggled up on the over-sized recliner we'd bought two weeks earlier. I was seated, the chair reclined, and Frost was settled sideways across my lap, nestled down low, her head resting on my shoulder and her feet dangling over the arm of the chair.

"So, that truck, I know that truck and I saw who got out. What did she want?"

I felt Frost tense slightly when Austin spoke, knowing that she was wondering how he knew about Celeste and how much he knew.

"Relax, baby, the truck used to be Brian's, Austin helped him fix it up ages ago before Brian left the Clipper pack. Austin, Becca and Abbey took those trips with us until Abbey and I turned ten, then they started staying behind to watch the pack, so they know Celeste too."

The explanation seemed to relax her a fraction, but that only earned me a raised eyebrow from Austin. I let out a huff and decided that I should probably just start from the beginning and explain everything to them. This was going to take a while and I hadn't ingested nearly enough coffee for the things this day had already brought down on me. I downed the rest of what was still in the mug in my hand and then gave Frost a smile when she moved to refill it for me. I took the mug back from her, gave her a moment to settle back into her place on my lap and then started talking. I began with that first crazy summer when I was twelve, walked them through the following two and then into the epiphany I'd had that resulted in the fight that ended everything.

Our friends sat and listened, not interrupting me as I laid the tale out for them, finally wrapping it up with a heavy sigh. I felt like I had just dropped fifty pounds and needed a nap for the effort, but that would just have to wait.

"Okay, so now she's back, all that jazz happened and, what? You think she's hoping she can just waltz back in and pick up where you left off when you were fifteen?"

"Sure seems that way to me, Abs."

"Well that's just nuts! Honestly, you have a mate, you're bonded for crying out loud! What does she think she's gonna do? Break you two up and take you for herself? Doesn't work that way and she should know that."

All I could do was nod slightly and give my best friend a look that expressed how crazy I thought this girl might be.

"I don't think she's really thinking that far ahead. I think she heard that Kyndle was fighting for a woman, to be with a woman and she figured she had to see it for herself. Maybe she never thought Kyn would actually be out about who she is and she was curious. Then she showed up and seeing her again made something flicker back to life."

Rebecca shrugged as she spoke and while she might be right, I had the feeling it was more than that. Unfortunately, I knew Celeste a bit too well to think that she hadn't shown up with some kind of motivation.

"I can't say I blame her, I don't know what I would have done if I'd ended up in her position."

Frost's words answered Rebecca's statement as they slipped out against my shoulder. I set my mug on the table beside the chair so I could wrap my arms around her and give her a reassuring squeeze.

"Be that as it may, she has no right to walk on this land, into this pack, and start causing trouble. When she comes back, she'll be dealt with. More than likely I'll just tell her she has to leave."

"What if she refuses?"

Abbey's question was a valid one and I just grinned a little and looked right at my best friend.

"Then she'll have my mate to deal with."

Frost grinned against my shirt and I felt her arm slide around my waist and squeeze tight.

"If she wants Kyndle, she'll have to go through me and believe me, she won't make it through me."

Frost wasn't typically the confrontational type so the thought of the sweet, passive woman on my lap getting in someone's face and taking them down over me was a little thrilling. In all honesty, it was a lot thrilling, the image of her putting Celeste in her place sent a shiver down my spine and pulled a soft rumble from my chest that I knew she felt when she giggled a little.

"What are you giggling about?"

Abbey looked utterly confused as Frost sat up and looked into my eyes, I was sure she was seeing the desire that was pooling low in my body reflected in them.

"Nothing you really want to know about Abbey, trust me."

My best friend huffed loudly and I knew an eye roll followed the sound without having to look. That was a good thing since I wasn't about to look away, the grin Frost was giving me promising that she was going to make sure I made up for the hurt I caused her earlier in the day. I was more than prepared to do exactly that, all night if she really wanted me too, it was a penance that I was thrilled to follow through with.

CHAPTER SEVENTEEN

I EASED one eye open against the sunlight streaming in through the gap in the blinds, remembering that we had, once again, forgotten to go buy actual curtains for the bedroom. It took me a moment to figure out why I was awake since the clock told me it was eight in the morning and we had intended to sleep until nine. The offending pounding on the front door brought the source to my attention and I growled as I rolled out from under Frost's arm and reached for my robe. I was still half asleep, but that was awake enough to remember that I shouldn't answer my front door naked. I slipped on the soft, powder blue robe and tied it closed as I shuffled to the bedroom door, yawning as I walked. I made my way down the hallway, leaving the bedroom door open as whoever was disturbing my sleep knocked again. Someone had better be dead or dying; I was exhausted and needed all the sleep I could get.

I reached the front door and looked through the small window in the solid wood, rolling my eyes and grumbling under my breath as I pulled it open. "What?"

"I'm really sorry about the other day, can we please talk?" It had been three days since Celeste had shown up at the house and sent my life into a moment of sheer chaos. I had actually started to hope that she had just left and we wouldn't be subjected to her interference any further. Dare to dream. I wasn't in the mood to deal with her again, not so early in the morning and I was about to say as much.

"I think you've said quite enough already, don't you? You need to leave." The voice from behind me interrupted my thought process and twitched a smirk onto my face. I stepped out of the way as Frost took my place in the door in a pair of my sweats and one of my tee shirts. I took a moment to admire how good her ass looked in my pants then leaned against her back, slipped my arms around her waist and rested my chin on her shoulder.

"I'm here to talk to Kyndle, not you." The venom in her voice when she spoke to Frost made me want to reach over and slap the shit out of her, but I reined in my temper as she turned her gaze to me. "Kyni, please, just talk to me. I'm just trying to understand what happened, where it all went wrong." I felt Frost tense in my arms at the nickname and then she took a deep breath and relaxed a fraction.

"I said you need to leave, Celeste. I'm asking you nicely, for the second time now. You won't get a third." The threat behind Frost's words hung in the air despite the civil tone that she had used, a tone that apparently made Celeste believe that she was bluffing. The smaller woman ignored her, imploring me with her eyes, but I ignored the look and turned my face into the soft skin of Frost's neck.

"Kyni..." The use of the offending nickname once again coupled with Celeste deciding to reach out and let her fingers brush my arm pushed Frost over the edge between civil and protective. She grabbed Celeste's arm with a harsh growl and I simply let my arms fall from her waist, giving her the space to move freely. Her other hand went to the collar of Celeste's shirt and she shoved the smaller woman backwards, right off our porch.

"Don't you dare touch her, you have no right."

Celeste had cowered for a moment, but seemed to take Frost's words as a challenge and jumped to her feet.

"No right? Oh honey, I thought you knew... I touched her first."

I could feel the tension pouring off Frost in waves and I started to wonder if I would have to keep her from actually killing Celeste. Running her off was one thing, but I couldn't let Frost have someone's death on her hands. I was barely handling the whole process, it would tear her apart. I relaxed just a bit when I heard my mate laugh, not her happy laugh, but something filled with ire and disdain.

"Nice try but I'm not falling for the bait. You may have held her hand first, you may have kissed her first, but even then, she wasn't yours. She saved herself for me, and you know what else?" I watched my mate step off the porch and down the steps into the snow barefoot, but showing no signs of being bothered by the cold. The smug looked steeled itself across Celeste's face as she crossed her arms over her chest and eyed Frost.

"What? What could you possibly say that would upset me?"

"You were the first, but I'll be the last. No one else will ever hold her the way I do, she's mine." Warmth I hadn't expected to feel erupted in my heart and spread over me as I watched the expression fall right off the smaller woman's face. Frost had hit her where it hurt and the declaration made a massive smile take over my face. I was hers, no matter what this crazy girl from my past tried, no matter what she said, Frost would never let me go. "Now get the hell off our land before I introduce you to our Enforcers." I heard the growl that carried the words and shivered a little, never having heard my sweet white wolf sound so angry. Celeste seemed to consider for a moment, almost as if thinking about pushing her further, but then decided against it. I looked on as she turned around, got into her truck and drove away, and then waited as Frost returned to the house and closed the door.

"That, my love, was sexy."

I watched her cheeks flush pink as a grin took over her features and I couldn't help but grin back.

"I don't know what came over me, I just got pissed when she touched you."

"Thank goodness you don't have my temper, eh?"

"Yeah, I might have knocked her into next week." I laughed because it was sadly true and she joined me for a few moments. My temper wasn't anything to laugh about, but we needed the mirth to dispel the tension that had gathered over the course of the confrontation. "Do you think that's the end of it? Have we seen the last of Celeste?"

"Hell no, that girl has never known when to give up. She'll be back." That made Frost huff and I just reached up and rested my palm against her cheek, my thumb brushing over her full lower lip. "It'll be okay, when she comes back, we'll deal with it. Nothing is going to come between us. Ever. Okay?" Our eyes locked and she nodded, knowing that I wasn't going anywhere, that she never needed to doubt how I felt about her. "Good, now come on, we're setting that damn alarm for ten and going the hell back to bed!" She laughed at me and then followed me back to the bedroom to crawl back under the covers for a bit longer. "Oh, and remind me to buy some fucking curtains."

"You and that mouth, woman." I paused as the words hit me then turned and pushed the door closed over her shoulder, pinning her against it, my lips so close to hers that any movement would bring them together.

"I didn't hear you complaining about my mouth last night." I felt it when her breath hitched a little then watched as the pale purple of her eyes deepened a couple shades, knowing that last night's activities were playing through her mind. A wicked little grin suddenly took over her mouth and in that moment, I knew that we wouldn't be getting that extra sleep I had wanted. I wasn't about to complain.

We stepped out of the house two and a half hours later, already five minutes late for our lunch date with Abbey and Kyle and found them waiting for us out front. Kyle was trying desperately to keep the smirk off his face while Abbey wasn't even attempting to hide hers. "I'm so glad we don't live with you two anymore. You know, for a quiet woman Frost, you get pretty noisy."

I glanced over at Frost in time to see her turn crimson a second before she tugged the hood on her sweatshirt up to cover her face. I couldn't help it, I burst out laughing which made Kyle lose his battle and join me. I was holding my stomach, a tear sliding down my cheek from laughing so hard when a snowball hit me in the ribs. It snapped me out of the laughter and drew my attention to my left, where Frost had a second white orb in hand, a smirk on her face.

"It's not nice to laugh at my embarrassment, sweetheart."

My jaw dropped a little as I stared at her, shocked that she had hit me with one of the icy balls.

"I can't believe you threw one of those at me." Her response was to chuck the other one in my direction, hitting me in the left thigh before I could get out of the way. "Oh, now you're gonna get it... Come here!"

I took off after her, but she was already running and had a head start, weaving and zig-zagging through the snow. Luckily, while she tended to be more agile than me, I was more athletic and could outrun her. It took me a couple minutes, but I finally managed to catch her and used my body weight to throw her off balance and pull her down into the snow. She landed on top of me, giggling like a maniac, her cheeks now flushed from the cold rather than embarrassment and slightly out of breath. She wiggled around until she turned over, looking down at me as I lay under her in the snow. I smiled up at her and she winked at me before she leaned down and brushed her lips over mine, just a moment of contact that I swear could have made the snow around us melt.

"Come on kids, we're gonna be late if we don't get moving!" Kyle's voice snapped us out of our moment, his words made me roll my eyes as Frost slipped off to one side and stood up. She offered me a hand to help me stand and then we brushed each other off before joining our friends by Abbey's truck.

"You know something Kyle? If you don't stop calling me kid, I might have to get nasty with you."

I picked up a handful of snow and plopped it on top of his head with a laugh before he could respond. He rolled his eyes, ruffled the snow from his hair and climbed into the truck with us. We made our way off pack land and toward the nearest town, meeting Austin and Becca there. We were sitting down to make some plans for the new pack, setting some rules, some boundaries and making plans for expanding the housing and getting the younger members into school. We met the last of our group outside the little diner and headed inside to get a table. The next three hours were spent eating and talking, coming to some agreements about things, including our new pack name. A pack needed a name, an identity, it was what gave us that sense of belonging, of family, of home.

Frost had remembered something I'd said at that last meeting with our old packs that had stuck with her. I had mentioned rising from the ashes, it had rooted itself in her mind and become a symbol for this new pack. We were like that mythical creature who, when its time had come, rather than dying, would burst into flame, releasing itself from its mortal bindings to rise from the ashes, to be born again new. We were the Phoenix pack, born again to rise and become strong once more. We all loved it and we had the feeling that the new pack would as well, for exactly the same reason. Several things planned out and decided, we finally left the diner so they could have their table back and started toward home. Abbey dropped Frost and I at our front steps and then turned the truck to head toward the house she and Kyle were sharing with Brandon, Tristan, August and the girls. We were just about to head inside when I stopped in my tracks, cocking my head to one side.

I held up a hand to stop Frost as she started to say something, listening for the small sound I had heard a moment before. I caught it again, turned toward my left and hopped down off the stairs to investigate which took me around the side of the house. I scanned the diamond-shaped openings in the decorative vinyl we had put up to enclose the underside of the porch and discovered a hole in it. I furrowed my brow slightly, and then heard the sound again, louder and clearer this time and my eyes went wide. "Frost! Come here, quick!" I heard her heading toward me so I didn't wait, just dropped down and slid under the porch as quickly as I could. I gave my eyes a moment to adjust in the awkward lighting in the small space and then saw what I knew I had heard. I turned and kicked at the vinyl, making the small hole bigger, knocking out the entire panel. I adjusted myself in the space and grabbed hold of the figure huddled in the dimly-lit space, pulling as I backed out into the cold. "Take her, get her inside." I handed the woman off to Frost who only looked shocked for a moment before coming to her senses and carrying the woman into the house.

I went back under the porch for the source of the noise I had heard, finding not one but two small bundles wriggling behind where the woman had been laying. I scooped them up, shimmied my way out from under the porch and made my way into the house. Frost had laid the woman out in front of the fire and was working on getting her boots off when I walked in. She turned, saw what I was carrying and her jaw dropped as she abandoned the woman for a moment to come make sure she wasn't seeing things. "Oh Kyndle, how long do you think they've been out there?"

"Under the porch or out in the cold?"

"Out there, in this weather."

"Too long, I'm sure. Let's get them warmed up." One of the small bundles began to cry and I handed the baby off to Frost who immediately started rocking the little one. I grabbed the phone and called Abbey, needing my Betas present on this one.

"Didn't we just drop you off? What did you forget this time?"

"Get over here, now. Bring your mom and dad." I hung up before she had the time to respond, but knew that she would rush right over, out of curiosity if nothing else. The two pairs stepped through the door a few short minutes later and froze at the entry into the living room. We had the woman settled in front of the fire, stripped out of her clothes that had been soaked through. We had replaced the wet clothing with a set of warm flannel, covered her with a blanket and slipped a pillow under her head. We had done what we could to dry and warm the babies as well, discovering that there was a boy and a girl. The little girl was soundly asleep in my chair near the fireplace while the boy was nestled in my arms since he cried every time we put him down.

"What on earth?" I looked at Rebecca and shrugged a little bit, not really sure what I could tell her about what she was seeing.

"I heard a noise from the side of the house when Abbey and Kyle dropped us off. I went to check it out and found a hole in the vinyl we put up so I slipped under the porch and found these three. She's been out since we brought her in, we're trying to warm her up, but it doesn't look good." I nodded toward the woman that I assumed was the mother of the two small children currently in my living room. They couldn't be more than a few weeks old and I was shocked that they weren't as bad off as their mother. The explanation seemed to be that she had been caring for them, feeding them, keeping them warm, and had neglected to do the same for herself. The other two couples settled in around the couch, Abbey holding the little girl as she slept, and we discussed what to do next. A whimper over by the fireplace made me hand the boy off to Frost as I slipped off the couch and over to the woman.

"Hey, you're okay. Do you know where you are?" Her eyes fluttered open and it seemed to take her a minute to focus on me. She glanced around the room and then settled on my face again before she tried to sit up. "Whoa, not so fast there, take it easy."

"The twins..." Her voice was raspy and cracked as she spoke, like she'd been coughing too much recently.

"We have them here with us and they're both fine from what we can tell." She seemed to relax a bit and laid back down on the rug we had placed her on. "What's your name?"

"Maggie." I gave her a small nod and then took the bottle of water that Kyle handed me, opening it and letting him drop the straw he was holding into it before I offered it to the woman. She drank some, coughed a little and then swallowed a bit more before she eased herself up so she was sitting.

"I'm Kyndle, that's my mate Frost."

When we talked to humans, I called Frost my wife, it was a term they recognized, but this woman wasn't human. I watched her glance between the two of us and if she had a problem with two females being mated, she didn't show it.

"That's Rail." She indicated the little girl resting peacefully in

Abbey's arms and then turned toward where Frost sat with the boy. "That's Rake."

"That's Abbey and over there is Austin, our Betas and their mates, Kyle and Rebecca." Each of them received a nod in greeting and again we heard no comments about our status. I stood again, needing to be on my feet so I could think since I had no clue what her answers to my coming questions might be. "What are you doing way out here?"

"I was looking for you."

"For us?" I watched her nod and handed her the water bottle when she reached for it, sat silent while she drank more and then waited for the reply.

"Yes, for you. I was part of the Shade pack." A set of four gasps went up around the room and Kyle exchanged a confused look with Frost.

"Brian's pack in Wyoming..." The two confused occupants of the room suddenly understood the reaction that we'd had to her confession.

"Not anymore, not for a while actually, Brian killed himself a few weeks after his mate was killed in a freak storm about a year ago." I felt like I might pass out and wavered a little, feeling Frost's arms around me, easing me to the floor after she had handed Rake off to Austin. I stared into the fireplace for a moment before I finally gathered myself and turned back to Maggie.

"I had no idea, no wonder Celeste showed up here dredging up the past."

"Celeste was here?" Maggie seemed like she was about to panic and I reached out and placed a hand on her shoulder to calm her.

"It's okay, she's gone now. Why the panic? What happened?"

"After Brian killed himself, his oldest son took over the pack. That didn't sit very well with most of the older pack members."

"Well why not? What did they have against West?" I watched her expression change as I mentioned the man's name, pain in her eyes as she looked down at her hands.

"He had taken a mate, the year before and the pack didn't like it. Brian allowed it but it never sat well with most of the older members."

"Why?"

"Mixed blood, they don't want 'mutts' in the pack." I looked at her, confusion on my face, not sure what to say until she looked up and decided to explain. "I'm not a werewolf, just a shapeshifter.

Canine, but only a shapeshifter." I shook my head and huffed out a heavy sigh, there was that wonderful judgmental nature our kind was so well known for.

"Okay, so what happened after Brian... After he passed."

"The pack found out I was pregnant and Felix challenged him. His own younger brother challenged him, can you believe it? They managed to put it off for a while, but eventually it happened and he won. He killed West... And ran me out not long after the twins were born." I felt Frost's arms tighten around me as my heart leapt into my throat and my breath caught. Maggie dissolved into a small coughing fit, drank a little more water and then took a shallow breath. "I didn't know where else to go. West talked about you a lot, he always said you were like a little sister to him. He knew about you and Celeste."

The news shocked me a little, he had never indicated that he had any clue about us, about me. The comment also made me shoot a slightly worried glance back at Frost, but thankfully she didn't seem affected by the mention of my former fling with the other girl. She was focused on Maggie.

"I really don't know why, but she never liked me, not even a little. Anyway, we had heard what happened with you right before West's challenge happened. The day after, Celeste disappeared, Felix took over and I was run out with two newborns to take care of. That was last week sometime, I'm not sure, I lost track of my days."

"Damn, what the hell is wrong with our species?"

I felt my mate shake her head against my shoulder as she spoke and knew that no one in the room had an answer to that question.

"I made it over the border and had almost reached where we had heard you were settling before my car broke down. I couldn't just sit there and freeze so I bundled the twins up as much as I could and started walking. Thank goodness I was only an hour walk from your fence line." I shook my head, an hour walk from our fence line meant that she had probably been walking in the snow for well over four hours, possibly as many as eight depending on where she had actually come through the fence. No wonder she looked so ragged and was coughing, I was again shocked that the twins seemed as healthy as they did.

"Well you're here now and we'll do what we can to take care of you and the twins." I nodded in agreement with Frost as Maggie offered us a smile before she started coughing again. "Come on, we'll get you settled into one of the spare rooms and then figure out getting the twins settled in." Kyle helped me get her up off the floor and down the hallway into the nearest spare room. Once she was settled and asleep, a couple bottles of water and some cough drops on the bedside table, Frost and I took over the babies and sent Austin and Kyle to buy a couple cribs and gather some supplies. They returned later that night and we cleared out half of the master closet for the cribs and a changing table, needing to have the twins where we could hear them since their mother might be in and out for a while. We spent the night rotating the babies between us while the four not holding them put together furniture and put things away.

Frost and I collapsed into bed just as the sun peeked through the gap in the curtains that I had finally remembered to buy and hang. I was exhausted and from the look of her, my mate was as well, it had been a long night. Maggie had only managed to wake up three more times over night, the first time informing us that Rake and Rail were only about eight weeks old. The second and third were only long enough to do some more coughing, the last fit leaving her barely able to breathe after she coughed up some blood. We were worried that she wouldn't make it and what that would mean for her two small children. Our kind didn't fall sick often, our immune systems stronger than those of humans but when we did get sick, it was typically debilitating and frequently fatal. We just couldn't do anything half-assed.

I was too tired to keep worrying about it just then and as I glanced over to see if Frost had anything to say, I found her already fast asleep. I smiled a little as I mustered the last of my strength, eased off the bed and tugged her shoes off, dropping them on the floor beside the bed. I undressed her down to her tee shirt and underwear and then shifted her enough to pull the blankets down and back over her. I undressed myself and crawled into my side of the bed, asleep almost before my head hit the pillow.

CHAPTER EIGHTEEN

I WHINED as I felt myself being shaken awake, a voice trying to break through the dark shield of sleep that I was clinging to like a life raft on the open ocean. I was still tired, I knew it without even waking up completely, the fog of exhaustion still firmly draped over my consciousness. I swatted at the hands gripping my shoulders, trying to get them to go away and let me get the sleep I needed. I adored that I got to sleep for a full eight hours these days and I was getting aggravated that someone wanted to interrupt that. I finally let out a sad whimper and slowly opened one eye, seeing Frost leaning over me from where she sat on the edge of the bed. I growled softly, grabbed the top of the blanket and rolled over, taking part of it with me and dragging it over my head. I wasn't getting up yet, I refused and there wasn't anything that she could say or do to make me.

"Kyndle, I know it's only been four hours baby, but you need to get up, it's Maggie." My eyes flashed open and I moved to sit up, knowing that there were only two reasons Frost would wake me on Maggie's account. I hoped to the gods that it was the better of the two outcomes as I slipped out of the bed and pulled on my sweat pants. We had found Maggie, Rake and Rail under our porch five weeks earlier and poor Maggie's health had been declining ever since. We were doing everything that we could to help her, but it was looking more and more bleak every day. She had called Frost and I into her room the week before and asked us to look after the twins if anything happened to her, that it was what their father would have wanted. It broke my heart, but I agreed, what else could I do?

I moved through the house, my mate on my heels and slid to a halt in my socks outside the smallest of our six bedrooms, the one we had made Maggie's room. I reached for the knob, but hesitated, not sure that I actually wanted to know what was happening on the other side of that wooden portal. Frost took the choice away from me when she reached around and turned the knob, pushing the door open on the scene inside. Kyle was standing in the middle of the room, his gaze distant, not focusing on anything in particular. He turned when he realized the door had opened and his brow furrowed down before he walked over and stepped past me out into the hallway.

I shifted my gaze to where Abbey was perched on the edge of the bed, bent over, shoulders jerking as she cried. I knew before she even looked over at me and spoke what had happened, but I let her say it anyway.

"She's gone, Kyndle."

The world slammed to a screeching halt around me and I had to remind myself that I needed to breathe, the action labored and pained. I'd known that she probably only had a short time left, but there had been a part of me that had hoped she would kick it, pull through and make it out the other side okay. It had been a hollow hope, whatever she'd been hit with was dug in deep. There was nothing any of us could do other than make her as comfortable as possible for the time she'd had left. I hoped we had managed that, but I didn't have time to dwell on it. We had made a promise to her and I had every intention of keeping it, no matter how difficult it would be.

The rest of our pack, now just over sixty strong since the rest of those who had left to follow us had shown up already knew about the mysterious shapeshifter who had shown up at our doorstep. We hadn't told them everything, knowing that there were parts that could wait until we knew what would happen with Maggie. Now that she had passed, we had some things to discuss with them, a few things to bring out into the open. I let out a heavy sigh and ran my hand through my hair as I tried to decide how to go about handling everything. Those thoughts were put on hold when I heard Frost sniffle behind me and I turned to find her crying quietly, leaned against the door frame.

I got hold of her hand and pulled her into a hug, giving her a few moments to break down without trying to talk her down. The times that Maggie had actually been lucid enough to talk to us she had proven to be a lot like my mate and they had started to become friends. I knew this would hit her hardest when it eventually happened and she would need some time to recover. She stood there and held onto me as she cried for a minute and then pulled in a deep breath and took a step back, her hands dropping into mine. She met my gaze and held it for a few seconds before she squeezed my hands and turned to Abbey, who had managed to calm down herself.

"We need to bury her, properly. She deserves that much."

Abbey and I both nodded our agreement and my best friend left the room, likely to find Kyle and start plans for taking care of that. I knew there were a couple things that Frost and I needed to talk about and I wasn't sure that waiting was the best option so I led her out of the room, closed the door gently behind me and then headed for our bedroom. I stepped into the space we had set up for the twins and picked up Rake who had started to whimper when he'd heard us come into the room. I turned to find my mate giving me a small, sad smile and I returned it as she reached over and brushed the baby's hair off his forehead.

"I know we never really took the time to talk about if we wanted this before we had it dropped on us..."

Her brow furrowed as she looked up at me, confusion on her pale features as she soaked in my comment.

"What do you mean? If we wanted what?"

"The whole family thing... We never really decided when, or even if we wanted kids. Now it looks like we've got two..."

She nodded as she looked back down at Rake, now settled and sleeping happily nestled in my arms and I watched the smile take over her face.

"I hate the circumstances. Obviously, I would have preferred it if Maggie could have recovered and raised them."

"That would have been ideal, yeah..."

"But she didn't, Kyn. And I don't know about you, but I'm not sure that I'd have it in me to give them up even if we hadn't promised her we'd take care of them."

"Got attached, huh?"

I let out a soft chuckle that didn't sound nearly as happy as I had hoped it would and she shook her head as she looked up at me.

"More than attached. Honestly... I love them, Kyndle. I want them here. With us."

The news managed to shock me some, not that I thought that my mate didn't like babies, I just hadn't been sure that she wanted any of our own. I shifted the baby in my arms enough to reach over and brush the backs of my fingers across her cheek. She looked back up at me as she stepped closer so I could wrap my arm around her. She touched a finger to Rake's little hand and he gripped it in his sleep, a soft cooing noise leaving him as he nuzzled his way in closer to me.

"And here is exactly where they'll stay. From here out, for better or worse, we're raising twins. Get used to being a mom."

The smile that took over her face at that threatened to stop my heart, the pure love in it as she watched him asleep in my arms apparent. It was just one more side of the woman that I loved I'd never seen before, and I already adored it. I managed to get Frost her finger back and settle Rake into his crib without waking him up so we could leave the room and go talk and let them sleep. We headed to the kitchen, finding Abbey and Kyle sitting at our table and a few silent hugs were exchanged. We all sat down and for a moment, no one said anything, but I finally broke the silence.

"We have to have a pack meeting, tell everyone. We were pretty vague about who she was and where she came here from before. I'd wanted to air on the side of caution in case Maggie recovered and didn't want everyone knowing her business. Now that she passed, we need to put it all out in the open for the pack. They deserve to know that we were harboring a non-wolf that was run out of another pack... And that the twins are part of the pack now, we're raising them as our own."

The looks Abbey and Kyle gave Frost and I at my comment were exactly what I had expected. We hadn't told them about the promise that Maggie had asked us to make, again having hoped that she would recover and it wouldn't matter.

"Really?"

Frost nodded at our Beta and I offered her a small smile when she grinned at me.

"Kyndle Callahan, a mom. Who would have ever guessed?"

"Me."

Abbey and I both focused on Frost who was smiling at me as she spoke. I raised a brow at her, not sure I believed that she had ever considered me being a mom before now.

"Oh, really?"

"Yeah, really. What, you think I never considered it? Just because we never really talked about it, doesn't mean I hadn't thought it."

"Aren't you just full of surprises?"

She let out a soft laugh and shook her head as she leaned her shoulder against mine.

"You'll make a great mom, Kyn. Just like you've made a great Alpha. You're kind and you care about people, you'll have the best interest of those two at heart their entire lives."

"Honestly... She's not wrong, Kyndle. I think this is the perfect next step for you."

I glanced between my mate and my best friend, feeling warm and as happy as I could given the circumstances that had led up to this conversation. Now we just had to hope the rest of our newly-formed pack would agree with them. We sent Abbey and Kyle to tell Austin and Rebecca what had happened and get the pack together for a meeting. It was late, but we needed to handle this as soon as possible so there was no better option than just getting it done and over with. Once they were on their way, we got ourselves together, making sure we were presentable before we bundled up the twins and headed out to the meeting space we had set up just after moving onto the property.

It didn't take long for the entire pack to filter into the space, most looking like they had been dragged out of bed for this. I felt a little guilty for getting them out in the middle of the night, but if our last year or so had taught me anything, it was that you couldn't put things off until the morning. You never knew what said morning would bring and it wasn't worth the risk. Once they were all gathered, Frost and I left the twins with Rebecca and Kyle and stepped up to address our pack together. They settled down to hear what we had to say quickly, all obviously curious about why they were gathered.

"Thank you all for hauling out here in the middle of the night, we appreciate it and I promise we would have let this wait until morning if we thought that was best. Some of you heard about the runaway that Frost and I took in a few weeks ago."

Nods and a few murmurs went through the gathered wolves and I pulled in a steadying breath to continue.

"She had defected from a pack in Wyoming that some of you

might actually know. The Shades. The short story is that their Alpha passed a bit back, his son took over with his mate and when the rest of the pack found out that she wasn't a werewolf, he was challenged, lost and she was run out."

The pieces started to click together for some of the pack, their expressions showing that they were understanding who it was we had taken in.

"Maggie was a shapeshifter, but that hadn't been good enough for the rest of the Shade pack. She was run off with her two newborns in tow and ended up here. How and why is a story for another time, but for now just know that she had her reasons. Recently, she realized that she might not make it and she asked Frost and I to take care of her twins if she died."

The fact that her death was so short a time before hit me again and my next couple breaths were a little ragged. Frost reached over and took my hand, lending me enough of her strength that I could continue.

"She passed tonight, and as we promised, Frost and I will be raising Rake and Rail here. They may only be half werewolf, but I want to make myself clear so please, listen carefully. As of tonight they are children of an Alpha pair, and part of this pack. Anyone who has a problem with that should speak up now..."

"Then allow me to voice my protest..."

CHAPTER NINETEEN

MY HEAD snapped toward the unfamiliar male voice, eyes narrowed to squint at the man over the flicker of the fire we had started to light the area. He stepped closer, his dark hair slicked back, black goatee perfectly groomed and determination in his unnervingly pale eyes. Austin and Abbey had been on their feet the moment they heard him speak, putting themselves between the intruding male and us, keeping Frost and I safely behind them. I was glad for their reaction time and the protection they were trying to offer, but I wasn't the kind of Alpha who would hide behind my Betas and Enforcers. I gave Frost's hand a squeeze and then stepped up between my two Betas, eyes narrowed at the man.

"And who are you that I should care?"

His chuckle was deep, unfriendly and sent a shiver down my spine that crawled its way right under my skin and made me want to wipe it off. Frost stepped up beside me, lending me her strength as my partner, my mate and I stared the man down, waiting for an answer.

"Name's Harlan."

He said it like it should mean something to me, but it wasn't familiar so I just stared back at him, waiting for more to go on than a name I'd never heard before. I crossed my arms over my chest after a moment and he huffed, apparently exasperated at me for not knowing who he was.

"I'm lead Enforcer for the Shade pack. Felix sent me to reclaim a couple of pack relatives you seem to have here."

I narrowed my eyes at him as my arms dropped back to my sides and I stepped a little closer.

"I don't know what you're talking about. You weren't invited and didn't announce that you were coming, therefor you're trespassing. You should leave."

"I'm not going anywhere, little girl."

I rolled my eyes at him for the comment, not sure why all of these men insisted on calling me that when they were trying to prove some kind of point. All it did was make them sound ridiculous, this one in particular since I was pretty sure he didn't know a damn thing about me. I took a moment to compose myself rather than snapping back at him and that gave me long enough to get a read on the scents surrounding us. I smirked at him and his eyes narrowed as I stepped in closer, hands finding my back pockets in a relaxed gesture that seemed to annoy him to no end.

"You should rethink that. You're alone, trespassing on Phoenix pack land and frankly, acting a bit threatening to their Alpha. That's not going to go well for you."

He barked out a single laugh and I wasn't sure if he was trying to bluff being more confident than he was or if was simply that stupid.

"You wouldn't dare do anything to me. It would bring the entire Shade pack down on you."

He had a point there, though I wasn't about to let him know it so I shrugged and then arced one brow at him.

"I actually don't really care at the moment. I'm still waiting to hear what you think you're doing here. All I've heard is what you were sent for, and that's not gonna go your way so... Why are you still here?"

That made him glare at me and I caught the movement of his hands clenching into fists at his sides for a moment before he relaxed them again and looked over my shoulder to where Kyle and Rebecca had Rake and Rail.

"Those little brats are our former Alpha's children. They don't belong here and Felix wants them back in Shade territory immediately."

"That's not happening."

"He's their only living relative and he will be taking them back."

"Over my dead body."

I smiled when Frost spoke up finally, giving her a quick glance and catching the fire flaring to life in her eyes as she stared the man down. Maggie may have just passed earlier in the day, but we had been caring for the twins for a while now, they were already ours. I wasn't sure that he had ever had the misfortune of provoking a she wolf protecting her family. If not, he had picked the wrong one to start with. She would rip him apart before she would let him touch a hair on their heads. He turned his glare on her with a growl and she let one loose right back at him when he tried to move around us.

She moved faster than he had expected, putting herself between his path and where Kyle and Rebecca had the twins. She had pure, protective rage in her gaze as she stared him down and even I was a little stunned when the man, almost twice her size, looked away and backed up a couple steps. A swell of pride rose in me as I watched her back him up a bit further from our little ones and I found myself glad that size meant nothing in this kind of standoff with our species. It wasn't about brute force in a stare down, it was about dominance and Frost had that in spades.

Once he was far enough away that he wasn't posing a direct threat to the twins anymore, she eased up a fraction and I stepped in. I put myself right behind her, my hand on her shoulder as I glared at him where he stood a few feet away.

"You aren't welcome here, none of your pack is. Leave, go tell Felix that he has no claim over the twins, Maggie wanted them here and that's where they'll be staying, with us. They're part of the Phoenix pack now, and if any of your wolves come anywhere near them, they'll have their mothers to deal with."

He looked like he was about to protest until Frost growled at him again and he raised both hands up in front of him in surrender as he backed up. All of his bluster and bravado had bled away and he had shown himself to be the lowly sub-Omega he really was. With one last flickering glance at the twins, he turned and left. Somehow, I doubted it would be the last that we heard from the Shade pack and Felix, but I knew that we would handle whatever they tried. Once he was out of sight and his scent was fading into the distance, I turned my attention back to our pack.

"Well that was exciting..."

A few of them chuckled and others grinned and shook their heads, but they all looked pleased at the way the situation had turned out. We put out the offer for anyone to speak up about the twins again and when there was no protest, we sent everyone back home to get some sleep. We did the same, desperately in need of some rest after the night we'd had. We were finally getting settled in and had even managed to get a couple more houses in the process of being built. Things were going pretty smoothly and if Harlan showing up and putting on a rather sad display at our pack meeting was our only speedbump, I would happily take it and move on.

CHAPTER TWENTY

AS IT turned out, there was more on the horizon for us than we had been prepared for. We had a short span of quiet, the progress on the property moving along at a steady pace as we got several more houses finished and families moved into their own spaces. Everyone had handled sharing living spaces well, but we could tell that they were all grateful to have their own homes again. With so many willing and able helpers to get things done, the work went quickly. Thanks to some friends we'd made in the city nearby, zoning and permitting was pushed through for each new building in record time. Before long, each family had their own home and in no time we had what amounted to a small village set up on the property.

Things had been calm, stable and that should have been my first indication that the other shoe was about to drop. Chaos seemed to rule my life the last couple years and no matter how hard I tried to steer clear of it, somehow it always managed to find me. With everything that could have happened, all the scenarios that could have played out, what actually happened wasn't something I had considered. I kept waiting for Felix to show up to try and take the twins or for Celeste to surface and start something again. As it turned out, reality had a much more twisted sense of humor and trouble followed on the heels of a small group of defects from our old packs who showed up to join us.

One of the five we took in was a familiar face. Her name was

Darla and she was the younger sister of Daniel, the crazed idiot who had been handed my former pack. She and her friends showed up at our property line late one afternoon, pleading with us to take them in. She had been worried that we might turn her away because of who her brother was, but she shouldn't have. I knew what he was like and I wasn't about to leave her out on her own when she was trying to get away from him. Hearing that he had just about run my old pack into the ground wasn't comforting, it made my heart ache a little, but there wasn't a damn thing I could do about it. The best I could do was offer the girls a place to call home so Frost and I welcomed them into our pack and got them settled in. It only took about two weeks for trouble to find us after that.

"Kyndle! Open the damn door!"

It was barely ten in the morning and I was doing my best to calm down a frantic Darla, currently curled up on one end of my couch in tears as her brother pounded on my front door. He had tracked her down and was livid that she was with Frost and I. He had shown up at the house she had been staying first looking for her and she had bolted out the back door, running right to our house to hide. He'd apparently caught her scent and followed her and she was terrified. Frost was sitting with her, trying to get her to relax a little and reassuring her that we wouldn't let anything happen to her. She was trembling and every time her brother pounded on the door or shouted through it, she jumped a little. It made me wonder if he hadn't subjected her to the same treatment I'd once put up with from Dane.

I wasn't about to open the door and risk him getting inside, though if he kept it up he might just break the thing down. I'd already called Austin and Abbey as well as August and two of our other Enforcers to come handle the situation, but my patience was beginning to wear thin. I had just pushed up to my feet when I heard the distinct tone of Abbey's voice through the door and I knew she had him distracted. I gave Frost's shoulder a squeeze and she glanced up at me.

I'm going outside to handle this... Are you okay with her?

She nodded, giving me a little smile when I used the mental link we had only just started communicating through recently to fill her in on my plan. I winked at her and then quickly let myself out the front door while Abbey and Austin had Daniel focused on them. I shut the door behind me and he turned where he stood in the middle of the yard, glaring when he saw me. He crossed back to the porch and took the steps in a single stride, putting himself right in my face. I didn't flinch, I hadn't ever really been scared of him and after the things I'd dealt with the last year or so he was only about as threatening as a biting fly. He snarled at me and I just blinked at him silently, refusing to let his posturing get to me, if he tried to back it up with actions, then I would react. For the moment, he was all bark and no bite.

"You need to leave, Daniel."

"I came to get my sister."

"Too bad, she's a Phoenix now and she's not going anywhere."

"Like hell she isn't. You have no right to keep her here."

"I'm not keeping anyone here. She came to us of her own free will. She's nineteen, she's an adult who made her choice and we're not about to hand her over to you."

He had barely managed to do more than twitch a muscle before he was locked in a sleeper hold and dragged from my porch. He struggled against the hold, but August had at least thirty pounds of muscle on him and wasn't about to let go. Bringing him with us and making him an Enforcer had been one of the best choices Frost and I had made. He was fiercely loyal and had a protective streak almost as wide as my mate's. Between the two of them, not a whole lot managed to get close enough to me to do any real damage. He showed no signs of letting the other man go and his struggles were getting weaker by the second as he crept closer and closer to blacking out.

"August."

He looked at me and I gave him a small, barely perceptible nod. Without another word or any argument on the matter, he released the other man. He took a small step back to let Daniel catch his breath and compose himself, but stayed close enough to grab him again if he tried anything. The sound of the door opening behind me caught my attention, but I didn't turn to look. I already knew that it was Frost with Darla, I'd heard them walking across the living room from where I was standing. My mate stepped up close to me, putting Darla between us and making sure that we could both get between she and her brother if he tried anything stupid.

"This entire pack is a joke. You aren't an Alpha. And she's nothing but a traitor."

He spit the last part toward Frost, eliciting a growl from me that pulled his attention back and when his gaze met my glare, he offered his own right back.

"Shut up. You don't get to even consider talking about her."

"Why? Because you don't wanna hear the truth? She interfered in a bonding that was signed off on by her Alpha, and yours and then stood back and watched as you killed her own brother. If that isn't a traitor, I don't know what is."

There was a point where that would have made me lose my temper and I would have laid him out for it. After everything we had been through, all it managed to do was make me laugh at him and shake my head. That served to piss him off and he growled at me, the sound making August take a step closer to him. I waved the younger wolf off, not needing him to step in, Daniel was ripping insults at us and I had the feeling that was because he knew that was all he had going for him.

"You're sure talking a lot for someone who started out so fired up. Unfortunately for you, my give a damn is running a little thin so unless you have something worthwhile to say, turn around and go home."

He bristled at that and as I finally really looked at him it hit me how ragged he looked. I frowned as I took in his appearance and then sighed and stepped down into the yard right in front of him. He puffed up a little, standing his ground as I circled him, getting a good scent track on him. By the time I stopped in front of him again, my expression was one part pity and two parts smug, a combination which made him bristle all over again.

"What the hell are you grinning at?"

"Let me ask you something, Dan... Did the pack turn on you after your own sister defected? Or was your leadership already failing by that point?"

That seemed to throw him a little and he faltered for a split second, recovering quickly, but I'd seen it and the damage had been done.

"I don't know what the hell you're talking about."

"Sure you don't... You don't actually care that Darla left. You really couldn't give a crap about anyone but yourself. But her turning her back on you was the last straw for some of the pack, wasn't it? Did they run you out? Or did you turn tail from a challenge and run like a sad little puppy?"

I was pushing his buttons now, actually trying to make him snap. I wanted to see what he still had in him, how far he had fallen. The fact was that while he was technically an Alpha, there were some who just didn't have it in them to lead. Not every Alpha handled themselves well and inherent dominance only took one so far before you had to prove yourself. An Alpha without respect, without the support of their pack was little more than an Omega on a power trip. I had the feeling that Daniel's dominance had faltered and that all this posturing was exactly that, nothing more than a show.

"Shut up, you little brat."

"I don't think so. Tell me something, do you think that dragging Darla back against her will to a pack she doesn't want will prove you deserve to lead? Do you think that will smooth things over and win you some respect? It won't... Because you haven't earned it and you don't deserve it. You say I'm not an Alpha, Daniel? I have a whole pack right there behind you ready to prove you wrong. Where's yours? You couldn't even manage to be dominate enough to get an Enforcer to do this for you, could you? Had to haul up to the great white north to do it yourself. So pathetic."

That did it, I finally pushed the right button and he snarled, lunging across the few feet between us at me. I sidestepped and brought my elbow down on his shoulder, knocking him face first into the dirt and then raised a hand at August to keep him from stepping in. I let him get back to his feet without offering any interference, I'd only put him down there in self-defense and I wasn't about to all out attack the guy. If he wanted to challenge me, I would gladly make sure he stayed down, but until then I would only defend myself. He pushed to his feet and turned toward me, anger plastered across his features as he let out a low growl.

"I hate you. What you did to the pack. You ripped the Clippers apart."

"No I didn't. My father did, when he refused to listen to reason and forced my hand."

"You killed him!"

"Yes, after he gave me no choice."

"You had a choice. You could have bonded with Cameron and shut the hell up. You should have. It was your place, but you just couldn't do what you were supposed to. You had to go and be rebellious. You say I don't care about anyone but myself. What about you, Kyndle? You shattered two packs, ripped apart dozens of families... For what? So you could have some stupid teenage fling?"

This time it was my turn to flinch, he'd managed to hit a bit of a nerve with the comment and I hated to admit that it stung a little.

He wasn't completely wrong, while what I had with Frost wasn't a fling by any stretch of the word, he had done exactly as he said. I glanced at August, living proof of what my choices had done to the families around me. He had lost everyone, everything because of the things I had done, something I had tried not to think about since we had left to start over months earlier. I knew Frost could feel me questioning myself through our bond, but as August met my gaze, I knew he could tell too, see it on my face.

"Don't let him get to you, Kyndle. Any damage that was done to the packs because of this wasn't on you and Frost. The two of you were putting things back together, making them better. Your father, Cameron and the council are to blame for the state the Clippers and the Riders are in now. Not you."

I smiled a little at him and felt a wave of pride wash through me from the bond, Frost's feelings tickling through my mind and bolstering me. They were right, it may have been my choices that set everything in motion, but I hadn't caused the bulk of the damage, I wasn't responsible.

"I didn't shatter the packs, Daniel. I can't speak to the condition the Riders were in before all of this, but I know for sure that the Clippers were already in trouble. They may not have known it, but my father was always one wrong comment away from losing it and ripping half the pack apart. No one ever knew because he took most of it out on me, and my brothers, but it was there all the same. I was trying to save everyone, make things right. If the pack has fallen apart, that's on you. You're their Alpha now, despite the fact that I told the council this would happen. You can't handle it, you may have been born an Alpha... But you have no clue what it means to lead. You're weak, and you don't deserve respect."

Done talking I turned my back on him and started to walk away, leaving an opening that he decided to try and take. He lunged at me again and was once again dropped to the dirt, though this time not by me or even August. I glanced over my shoulder and smiled at Frost as she pressed her sneaker between his shoulder blades, keeping him pinned for a few seconds before she backed away and let him up. Once he was on his feet, he rounded on her, but the look on her face stopped him dead in his tracks.

"I do my best to not be violent, Daniel, but I can promise you this, try that again and next time I'll make damn sure you don't get back up."

Something in her eyes must have shown him how serious she

was because after a few long seconds of staring each other down, he turned and practically bolted from the yard. I nodded to August and he turned to follow the other man, Austin and Abbey right behind him. They would make sure that he left our property and if he tried anything sneaky, they would handle it. I trusted the three of them completely. As they vanished, I turned to Darla who looked less frantic and panicked than she had at the beginning of the whole ordeal. She smiled at me as Frost stepped up beside me and slipped her arm around my waist.

"Thanks. Both of you. I hope it's still okay that I stay here."

"Of course, Darla this is your home now and we're your family. We'll always defend you."

She beamed at Frost for the words and I couldn't help myself, I pulled her in close and kissed her, ignoring the teasing wolf whistle from Kyle and one of my brothers making gagging noises. We parted and everyone dispersed, heading back to their homes to get back to whatever they had been doing before the whole scene had started. Frost and I sent Darla on her way and then shuffled back into the house, glad that somehow the twins had managed to sleep through the entire ordeal. We had just settled onto the couch to relax when there was a knock on the door and I groaned. I had learned to tell the knocks of several pack members apart and this one was familiar.

"Come in Austin, this better be good."

He made his way into the living room, a serious look on his face that made me sit up a little straighter and pay attention.

"Daniel tried to circle back around and come back. Don't worry, we managed to catch him and run him off..."

"But?"

"But... Before he left, he dropped some news on us. I didn't believe him so as we were headed back, I called Hank to check in and he confirmed it."

"What?"

Whatever it was it must be pretty bad for Austin to be skirting the subject the way he was. I didn't know if I really wanted to know, but as Alpha, I needed to.

"The council of the northwest territory packs is pushing to go public."

"You're kidding me, right?"

"I wish I was. They've got plans to make Greg the face of the packs and out us to the world. We just don't know when."

ABOUT THE AUTHOR

Kaden is an Arizona based author currently living north of Phoenix with their wife and small zoo of pets. They love all things nerdy and can regularly be found playing board and table top games, writing new D&D campaigns, browsing through the nearest convention or listening to true crime podcasts.

Conquest: Kai's Story

2017 Rainbow Awards Honorable Mention

"This story is extremely well written, the plot flows effortlessly, it made me feel, the characters come to life, I hated having to put it aside to get on with real life. In short, Conquest ticked all the boxes that make a book a top-notch read for me." - Dee England

In the late 24th century, life seemed to be going well for the human population of Earth. War, famine, debt, and disease had been eradicated and a new era of peace and discovery was ushered in. However, as history has taught us over and over again, there is rarely a rise without a corresponding fall.

When a new technology which brought free, clean energy to all of mankind failed, the planet and its human population suffered great loss. With most of the people once inhabiting the planet dead or dying, a new time of human rose to the place of survival: the Regen. Able to use the deadly radiation leaked into Earth's flora, fauna, and atmosphere as a healing agent, the Regens constantly regenerate their cell structure. The result is a lack of radiation-caused disease and lengthened lifespans.

However, each and every human being must have its opposite and for the Regens this meant the Purists. Average humans who were somehow immune to radiation poisoning and other effects. Taking up their side against the Regens and labeling them evil, a new era of struggle, powerplays, and fighting dawned.

Follow four Regen Resistance Generals in their quest to be named as equals to the Purists. Each General, giving a nickname by the Purist leaders, represents one of the Four Horsemen of the Apocalypse. Meet Kai, known by her enemies as Conquest, in this first installment of a set of four novels.